THE SEAGULL.

ANTON CHEKHOV.

THE SEAGULL.

ANTON KORENEV.

A comedy in four acts.

Anton Korenev Entertainment.

MMXXI.

© 2021 Anton Korenev

All righs reserved. For permissions and licensing contact
publishing@antonkoreneventertainment.com.

Ч is the exclusive trademark and service mark of Anton Korenev Entertainment.
The moral rights of Anton Korenev have been asserted.

Publisher's Cataloging-in-Publication Data:

Names: Chekhov, Anton Pavlovich, 1860-1904, author.
  | Korenev, Anton Sergeyevich, 1977-, author.
Title: The seagull / Anton Pavlovich Chekhov, Anton Sergeyevich Korenev.
Description: Knoxville, TN : Anton Korenev Entertainment, 2021.
Identifiers: LCCN 2020946434 | ISBN 978-1-953608-00-0 (hardcover)
  | ISBN 978-1-953608-01-7 (paperback)
Subjects: LCSH: Chekhov, Anton Pavlovich, 1860-1904--Translations into English.
  | BISAC: DRAMA / Russian & Former Soviet Union. | FICTION / Classics.
  | LITERARY COLLECTIONS / Russian & Former Soviet Union.
Classification: LCC PG3456.C5 .K67 2021 | DDC 891.72/3--dc23

Published by Anton Korenev Entertainment: antonkoreneventertainment.com.

CONTENTS.

PREFACE. vii
CHARACTERS. xi
THE SEAGULL. 1
    ACT ONE. 3
    ACT TWO. 43
    ACT THREE. 69
    ACT FOUR. 101
ADDITIONAL MATERIALS. 141

PREFACE.

PREFACE.

The kick-off meeting for *The Seagull* theatrical production was held in New York City in early April 2019. Almost a year later the production was finally about ready to be offered to the public, only to be put on pause after the pandemic's arrival and the shutdown of theaters for an indeterminate time . . .

Meanwhile, one of my tasks was to make the production accessible to the English-speaking audience. The challenge was the desire to use the Russian language from the end of the 19th century to reproduce the sounds, melody, and poetics of the spoken language that Anton Chekhov had originally intended. The obvious solution was to add English captions during the performance, and that was the first motivation to translate the play.

At the same time, with in-person rehearsals on hold, the actor in me felt the frustration growing. For months I had been asking myself what I could do to better understand the character of Trigorin, the writer. The answer seems obvious in hindsight: to write or, in my case, to translate. That overdue insight provided the second reason to work on this translation.

Please note that I ended up slightly restructuring the stage directions to improve readability, at least as I see it, but their content still almost always matches Chekhov's original remarks. The stage directions in the theatrical production have been modified a little more to immerse the audience into the atmosphere of a Chekhovian estate in 1896.

PREFACE.

Ч, the trademark and service mark for our undertakings related to *The Seagull*, is both a letter in the Russian alphabet and a number.

The letter, pronounced as [ch], is the first letter of the following relevant words in Russian:

- the family name of the playwright;
- the name of the play [cháika];
- the family name of the composer Pyotr Tchaikovsky, a contemporary and friend of Anton Chekhov, whose music is used extensively in the theatrical production;
- the word for the number four [chetýre].

The number symbolizes:

- the four acts;
- the four seasons corresponding to each of the four acts;
- the four movements of a symphony;
- the four characters whose lives intertwine the most.

Anton Korenev,
2021.

CHARACTERS.

CHARACTERS.

Irina Nikolayevna A R K A D I N A (Trepleva by marriage), an actress.

Konstantin Gavrilovich T R E P L E V (Kostya), her son.

Pyotr Nikolayevich S O R I N (Petrusha), her brother.

N I N A Mikhaylovna Zarechnaya, daughter of a rich landowner.

Ilya Afanasyevich S H A M R A Y E V, a retired lieutenant, SORIN's estate manager.

P O L I N A A N D R E Y E V N A, his wife.

M A S H A (Marya Ilyinichna, Mashenka), his daughter.

Boris Alekseyevich T R I G O R I N, a belletrist.

Evgeniy Sergeyevich D O R N, a doctor.

Semyon Semyonovich M E D V E D E N K O, a teacher.

Y A K O V, a worker.

C O O K.

M A I D.

THE SEAGULL.

ACT ONE.

Part of the park on SORIN's estate. A wide alley, leading deep into the park toward the lake, is obstructed by a platform, hastily assembled for an at-home performance, so that the lake cannot be seen at all. Bushes to the left and to the right of the platform, several chairs, a small table.

The sun has just set.

THE SEAGULL.

(YAKOV and other workers are on the platform behind the closed curtain, coughing and hammering. MASHA and MEDVEDENKO enter from the left, returning from a stroll.)

MEDVEDENKO

—Why do you always wear black?

MASHA

—It shows that I am mourning my life. I am unhappy.

MEDVEDENKO

—Why? I do not understand . . . You are healthy, your father, even though he isn't rich, is wealthy enough. Life is much harder for me than it is for you. I am getting only 23 rubles a month, and that is before they take out my retirement contribution, and yet I do not wear mourning clothes. (Both sit down.)

MASHA

—It is not about money. A poor man can still be happy.

MEDVEDENKO

—That's in theory, but in practice it comes out like this: me and my mother, then two sisters and a little brother, and the salary is only 23 rubles. We need to eat and drink, right? Need tea and sugar, right? Need tobacco, right? Gotta keep spinning.

MASHA

—(turns toward the platform) The performance starts soon.

ACT ONE.

MEDVEDENKO

—Right. Performed by Zarechnaya, and the play is composed by Konstantin Gavrilovich. They are in love with each other, and today their souls will merge in the aspiration to present one and the same artistic image. Yet my soul and yours do not have any common points of contact. I love you, cannot sit home with my longing, every day I walk six kilometers on foot to get here and then six kilometers to get back and am greeted with the same indifferentism on your part. It is understandable. I do not have resources but have many relatives to take care of . . . What's the desire to marry a man who cannot even feed himself?

MASHA

—Nonsense. (Snuffs tobacco.) Your love touches me, but I cannot answer with reciprocity, that is all. (Holds out her snuffbox to MEDVEDENKO.) Take some of this.

MEDVEDENKO
—Don't feel like it.

(Pause.)

MASHA

—It is humid, must be a thunderstorm coming on tonight. You keep philosophizing or talking about money. According to you there is no greater misfortune than poverty, but I think it is a thousand times easier to wear rags and to scrounge around than . . . Anyway, you would not understand this . . .

(SORIN, leaning on his cane, and TREPLEV enter from the right.)

S O R I N
—It feels, my friend, kind of odd to live here in the country, and obviously I will never get used to it. Yesterday I went to bed at ten and this morning woke up at nine with such a feeling as though after a long sleep my brain was stuck to my skull and such. (Laughs.) And after lunch I accidentally fell asleep again, and now I am absolutely shattered, experiencing a nightmare, after all . . .

T R E P L E V
—Really, you need to live in the city.
—(notices MASHA and MEDVEDENKO) Dear friends, when it starts, somebody will call you, you cannot stay here. Leave, please.

S O R I N
—Marya Ilyinichna, would you be so kind as to ask your old man to arrange for someone to untie the dog, otherwise it keeps howling. My sister has not slept all night again.

M A S H A
—Talk to my father yourself, but I am not going to. Leave me out of it, please.
—(to MEDVEDENKO) Come on!

MEDVEDENKO

—(to TREPLEV) Do not forget to send for us before the start.

(MASHA and MEDVEDENKO exit.)

SORIN

—That means the dog will howl all night again. What a story, never have I lived in the country the way I wanted to. I used to take 28-day vacations and come down here to rest and such, but instead you would be hassled so much over various nonsense that ever since the first day you would want to get out. (Laughs.) Always have I left this place with pleasure... Well, and now I am retired, there is nowhere else to go, after all. Whether you want to—or do not want to, you have to keep on living...

YAKOV

—We are going to swim, Konstantin Gavrilovich.

TREPLEV

—Very well, just be back in your places in ten minutes. (Looks at his watch.) It starts soon.

YAKOV

—Will do.

(YAKOV exits.)

T R E P L E V

—And this is the theater. The curtain, then the first wing, then the second, and the rest is the empty space. No decorations whatsoever. Only the view of the lake and the horizon straight ahead. We'll pull up the curtain exactly half an hour before nine when the moon is already up.

S O R I N

—Magnificent.

T R E P L E V

—If Zarechnaya is late, then of course the whole effect will be lost. It's time for her to be here. Her father and stepmother keep her under guard, and it is as difficult for her to leave the house as it is to break out of prison. (Fixes SORIN's tie.) Your hair and beard are disheveled. Maybe you need to trim them, or something . . .

S O R I N

—(fixing his beard) The tragedy of my life. Even in my youth I had this appearance as though I had been drinking nonstop and such. Women have never loved me. (sitting down) Why is the sister in such low spirits?

T R E P L E V

—Why? She is bored. (sitting down by SORIN) She is envious. She is already against me, and against the performance, and against my play because it is not she who is performing but Zarechnaya. She does not know my play, but she already hates it.

ACT ONE.

SORIN

—(laughs) You're making things up, really . . .

TREPLEV

—She is already annoyed that on this little stage Zarechnaya will have success and not her. (Looks at his watch.) A psychological peculiarity—my mother. Indisputably talented, intelligent, able to sob over a book, can masterfully recite all of Nekrasov by heart for you, takes care of people who are sick like an angel; but I dare you when she is around to even try praising Duse! Oh-ho-ho! It's necessary to praise only her alone, necessary to write about her, to scream, to be excited about her extraordinary performance in *La Dame aux Camélias* or in *The Delirium of Life*, but since here, in the country, there's no such stupefying substance, that's why she is bored and angry, and we all—her enemies, we all are guilty. Then she is superstitious, afraid of three candles, the number thirteen. She is stingy. She has seventy thousand in a bank in Odessa—I know that for sure. But you ask her to lend you money, she will start crying.

SORIN

—You've imagined that your play will not appeal to your mother, and you already are nervous and such. Calm down, your mother adores you.

TREPLEV

—(tearing petals off a flower) Loves me—loves me not, loves me—loves me not, loves me—loves me not. (Laughs.) You see, my mother does not love me. What else is new! She wants to live, to love, to wear luminous jackets, but I'm already 25 years old, and

I'm a constant reminder that she is no longer young. When I'm not there, she is only 32, yet when I am around, she is 43, and for that, she hates me. She is also aware that I do not accept theater. She loves theater, it seems to her that she is serving humanity, a sacred art, but I think the modern theater is—a routine, a superstition. When the curtain goes up and under evening illumination, in a room with three walls, these great talents, the priests of that sacred art portray how people eat, drink, love, walk, wear their jackets; when they try to fish for a moral in the most tasteless scenes and phrases—some minuscule, easily digestible moral that could be put to some practical use at home; when in a thousand variations they keep presenting me with always the same thing, always the same thing, always the same thing—then I run and run, like Maupassant ran away from the Eiffel Tower that was pressing down on his brain with its vulgarity.

S O R I N
—We cannot be without theater.

T R E P L E V
—We need new forms. New forms are what we need, and if there aren't any, then it's better we do not need anything at all. (Looks at his watch.) I love my mother, love her dearly; but she leads a pointless life, always busy with that belletrist, newspapers keep flapping on about her—and that tires me out. Sometimes it's simply the egoism of an ordinary mortal in me speaking; on occasion I pity myself because my mother is a famous actress, and it seems that had she been an ordinary woman, then I would be happier. Uncle, what could be more desperate and ridiculous than this setup: she used to have guests over, every single one a celebrity,

artists and writers, and among them only I was—a nothing, and I was tolerated solely because I was her son. Who am I? What am I? Had to quit the third year of university for reasons, as they say, beyond editorial control, no talents whatsoever, not even a half kopeck of money, and the passport reads that I am—a tradesman from Kiev. Since my father was a tradesman, even though he too was a famous actor. Anyway, when all those artists and writers, sitting in her living room, were occasionally paying me some of their gracious attention, it seemed that with their eyes they were just measuring my nothingness—I could guess their thoughts and suffered the humiliation.

SORIN
—By the way, tell me, please, what kind of person is that belletrist? You cannot quite understand him. He keeps silent.

TREPLEV
—An intelligent, simple man, a little, you know, melancholic. Very upstanding. It's going to be a while before he turns 40, but he is already famous and spoiled by life's successes . . . As for his writings, they are . . . how can I say it? Amusing, talented . . . but . . . after Tolstoy or Zola you do not want to read Trigorin.

SORIN
—But I, my friend, love writers. Back in the day I passionately wanted two things: wanted to marry and wanted to become a writer, but was not lucky enough to do one or the other. Right. Even being a minor writer must feel good, after all.

THE SEAGULL.

TREPLEV

—(listens closely) I hear footsteps . . . (Hugs SORIN.) I cannot live without her . . . Even the sound of her footsteps is beautiful . . . I'm so happy, I could go insane.

(NINA enters.)

TREPLEV

—(quickly walks toward NINA) Magical fairy, my dream . . .

NINA

—(anxiously) I am not late . . . Of course I am not late . . .

TREPLEV

—(kissing NINA's hands) No, no, no . . .

NINA

—I've been restless all day, I was so scared! I was afraid my father would not let me come here . . . But he just left with my stepmother. The sky is red, the moon has already started to rise, and I urged my horse on, urged it on. (Laughs.) But I am glad. (Firmly shakes SORIN's hand.)

SORIN

—(to NINA, laughs) The eyes seem to have tearstains . . . He-he! That is no good!

ACT ONE.

NINA

—That is true ... You see how hard it is for me to breathe. I am leaving in half an hour, we need to hurry. I can't, I can't, in the name of God, do not delay me. My father doesn't know that I am here.

TREPLEV

—Indeed, it's already time to start. We need to call for everyone.

SORIN

—I will go and such. Right this minute. (Starts walking to the right and sings) "To France were the two grenadiers ..." I remember once I started singing, and one deputy prosecutor said to me: "You have, your excellency, a powerful voice ..." Then he paused to think and proceeded: "But ... poor for our ears." (Laughs.)

(SORIN exits.)

NINA

—My father and his wife do not let me come near here. They say it is bohemia ... afraid that I might choose to become an actress ... But I am being drawn here to the lake, like a seagull ... My heart is filled with you. (Looks around.)

TREPLEV
—We're alone.

NINA

—Seems to be someone there . . .

TREPLEV

—Nobody is there. (A kiss.)

NINA

—What sort of tree is this?

TREPLEV

—An elm.

NINA

—Why is it so dark?

TREPLEV

—It's already evening, all objects darken. Do not leave early, I implore you.

NINA

—I can't.

TREPLEV

—What if I follow you, Nina? I will stand all night in the garden and look at your window.

ACT ONE.

NINA

—You can't, you will be caught by a watchman. Trezor is not used to you yet and will bark.

TREPLEV

—I love you.

(YAKOV quietly enters.)

NINA

—Sh...

TREPLEV

—Who's there? Is that you, Yakov?

YAKOV

—(from behind the platform) That's right.

TREPLEV

—(to YAKOV) Take your places. It's time. Is the moon rising?

YAKOV

—That's right.

TREPLEV

—Is the alcohol ready? Is the sulfur ready? When the red eyes appear, it's necessary to have the smell of sulfur.

—(to NINA) Go, everything there is ready. Are you nervous?

NINA

—Very much so. Your mother—it's nothing, I am not afraid of her, but you have Trigorin . . . To perform in front of him, I am scared and ashamed . . . A famous writer . . . Is he young?

TREPLEV

—Quite.

NINA

—He has such marvelous short stories!

TREPLEV

—(coldly) Don't know, have not read him.

NINA

—Your play is difficult to perform. There are no live characters in it.

TREPLEV

—Live characters! Life needs to be portrayed not as it is, and not as it must be, but as it is being presented in dreams.

NINA

—Your play has little action, only a recitation. And in a play, I think, there must certainly be a place for love . . .

(NINA and TREPLEV go behind the platform.)

ACT ONE.

(POLINA ANDREYEVNA and DORN enter.)

POLINA ANDREYEVNA
—It is starting to get humid. Come back, put on your galoshes.

DORN
—I am hot.

POLINA ANDREYEVNA
—You are not taking care of yourself. This is stubbornness. You are—a doctor and know perfectly well that humid air is harmful for you, but you prefer that I suffer; you deliberately spent the whole evening yesterday out on the terrace . . .

DORN
—(sings quietly) "Don't say to me that youth of yours is ruined . . ."

POLINA ANDREYEVNA
—You were so involved in a conversation with Irina Nikolayevna . . . you did not even notice the cold. Admit it, you're attracted to her . . .

DORN
—I'm 55 years old.

POLINA ANDREYEVNA
—Nonsense, that is not an old age for a man. You've kept yourself up perfectly well and are still attractive to women.

THE SEAGULL.

DORN

—Then what else do you need?

POLINA ANDREYEVNA

—You all are willing to fall on your knees in front of an actress. All of you!

DORN

—(sings quietly) "Enchanted again, I am standing before you . . ." If society loves artists and relates to them differently than to, for instance, tradesmen, then that's the proper order of things. That is—idealism.

POLINA ANDREYEVNA

—Women have always been falling in love with you and throwing themselves at you. Is that also idealism?

DORN

—(shrugs his shoulders) I guess, so? There was much that was good in the way women related to me. They predominantly loved the superb doctor that I was. About 10, 15 years ago, you remember, I was the only upstanding obstetrician in the whole governorate. And then I've always been an honest person.

POLINA ANDREYEVNA

—(grabs DORN's hand) My dear!

DORN

—Quiet. They're coming.

ACT ONE.

(ARKADINA and SORIN arm in arm, TRIGORIN, SHAMRAYEV, MEDVEDENKO and MASHA enter.)

SHAMRAYEV
—(to ARKADINA) In 1873 at the Poltava Fair her performance was just amazing. Genuine excitement! Wonderful performance! Would you also happen to know where the comedic actor Chadin, Pavel Semyonovich, is these days? He was inimitable as Rasplyuev, better than Sadovskiy, I swear to you, dearest. Where is he these days?

ARKADINA
—You keep asking about those people from before the Flood. How do I know! (Sits down.)

SHAMRAYEV
—(sighs) Pashka Chadin! You will not find those people these days. The stage has fallen down, Irina Nikolayevna! There used to be mighty oaks, and now we see only the stumps.

DORN
—Brilliant prodigies are few now, that is true, but the average actor is at a much higher level.

SHAMRAYEV
—Cannot agree with you. In any case, it's a matter of taste.
De gustibus aut bene, aut nihil.

(TREPLEV comes out from behind the platform.)

ARKADINA
—My darling son, when exactly is the beginning?

TREPLEV
—In just a minute. Patience, please.

ARKADINA
—(from *Hamlet*) "My Son! You've turned my eyes inside my very soul and made me see in it such bleeding, deadly ulcers—and left me no salvation!"

TREPLEV
—(from *Hamlet*) "And why have you succumbed to vice and looked for love in the abyss of the crime?"

(A *rozhok* is played behind the platform.)

—Dear friends, the beginning! Attention, please!

(Pause.)

TREPLEV

—I begin. (Knocks with a little stick, then loudly) O you, the venerable old shadows that race at nighttime above this lake, put us to sleep and let us see in our dreams what will be in two hundred thousand years!

SORIN

—In two hundred thousand years there will be nothing.

TREPLEV

—Then let them portray for us what that nothing will be.

ARKADINA

—Let's. We're asleep.

(The platform curtain goes up; the view of the lake opens; the moon is above the horizon, its reflection on the water; on a large rock sits NINA, all in white.)

NINA

—Men, lions, eagles and partridges, horned deer, geese, spiders, silent fish that used to dwell in water, sea stars, and those not visible to the naked eye—in other words, all forms of life, all forms of life, all forms of life, having accomplished a sad circle, have faded away . . . It has already been thousands of centuries since Earth has carried a single living creature, and this poor Moon needlessly lights its lantern. In a meadow cranes no longer wake up with a scream, and May beetles can no longer be heard in linden groves. So cold, cold, cold. Empty, empty, empty. Scary, scary, scary.

(Pause.)

—The bodies of the living creatures have perished into particles, and eternal matter has turned them into stones, into water, into clouds, and the souls of them all have merged into one. The collective world soul—it is I . . . I . . . Within me are the souls of Alexander the Great, and Caesar, and Shakespeare, and Napoleon, and the last leech. Within me the consciousnesses of the men have merged with the instincts of the animals, and I remember everything, everything, everything, and each life within myself I relive once again.

(The ghost lights of the lake appear.)

ARKADINA

—(quietly) This is something decadent-ish.

TREPLEV

—(imploringly, with reproach) Mother!

NINA

—I am lonely. Once in a hundred years I open my lips so I can speak, and my voice sounds in this emptiness gloomily, and no one can hear . . . And you, the pale lights, cannot hear me . . . By early morning you are delivered by the festering lake, and you wander until dawn, but without thought, without volition, without the flutter of life. Afraid that some life-form would awaken within you, the father of eternal matter, the devil, every instant within you, as well as within the stones and the water, performs an exchange of atoms, and you are changing uninterruptedly. What stays constant and invariable in the universe is the spirit.

(Pause.)

—Like a prisoner thrown into a deep empty well, I do not know where I am and what is waiting for me. What is not hidden from me is that in this relentless, brutal fight with the devil, the source of material forces, I am destined to prevail, and afterward the matter and the spirit will merge in a beautiful harmony, giving rise to the kingdom of world volition. But that only will be, when little by little, over a long, long series of millennia, this Moon, and this luminous Sirius, and this Earth turn to dust . . . And until then, horror, horror . . .

(Pause.)

(Two red dots appear against the backdrop of the lake.)

—There is my mighty opponent, the devil, approaching. I see his scary blood-red eyes . . .

ARKADINA

—It smells of sulfur. Is that necessary?

TREPLEV

—Yes.

ARKADINA

—(laughs) Yes, quite an effect.

TREPLEV

—Mother!

NINA

—He is bored without a human being . . .

POLINA ANDREYEVNA

—(to DORN) You took your hat off. Put it on, or you will catch a cold.

ARKADINA

—The doctor took his hat off in front of the devil, the father of eternal matter.

TREPLEV

—The play is over! Enough! Curtain!

ACT ONE.

ARKADINA
—What are you angry about?

TREPLEV
—(flaring up, loudly) Enough! Curtain! Give me the curtain! (Stomps his foot.) Curtain!

(The platform curtain comes down.)

—My fault! I let it out of my sight that writing plays and performing on the stage are available only to the chosen few. I infringed upon the monopoly! I am ... I ... (Wants to say something else, but waves his hand instead.)

(TREPLEV exits to the left.)

ARKADINA
—What's with him?

SORIN
—Irina, that's not the way, my dear, to treat the young ego.

ARKADINA
—Was it something that I said?

SORIN
—You've offended him.

ARKADINA

—He himself warned that this was a joke, and I've been treating his play like a joke.

SORIN

—Still . . .

ARKADINA

—Now it turns out that he has written a literary masterpiece! Please! That means he has put on this spectacle and perfumed us with sulfur not as a joke but as a demonstration . . . He wanted to teach us about how one needs to write and what is necessary to perform. In the end, this is starting to get boring. I don't know what you think, but these constant forays against me and pinpricking would bore anybody! A capricious boy with a big ego.

SORIN

—He wanted to please you.

ARKADINA

—Really? And yet he did not choose some ordinary play but instead forced us to listen to this decadent nonsense. For the sake of a joke I'm willing to listen even to nonsense, but here we have claims for new forms, for a new era in art. While I think there are no new forms here whatsoever, just plain poor character.

TRIGORIN

—Each writes the way they want and the way they can.

ACT ONE.

ARKADINA
—Let him write the way he wants and the way he can as long as he lets me alone.

DORN
—Jupiter, you are angry . . .

ARKADINA
—I am not a Jupiter, I'm a woman. (Lights a cigarette.) I am not angry, I'm just annoyed that the young man is spending his time in such a boring fashion. I did not want to offend him.

MEDVEDENKO
—No one has a basis to separate the spirit from matter since it may be that the spirit itself is an aggregate of material atoms.
—(to TRIGORIN, lively) And you know what, maybe one could describe in a play and then perform on the stage the life of— my fellow teacher. A difficult, difficult life!

ARKADINA
—That's fair, but let's not talk about either plays or atoms. Such an outstanding evening! Do you hear, my dear friends, the singing? (Listens closely.) It's so good!

POLINA ANDREYEVNA
—That's on the other side.

(Pause.)

ARKADINA

—(to TRIGORIN) Sit by me. Some 10, 15 years ago here at the lake, music and singing could be heard uninterruptedly almost every night. There are six country estates around the lake. I remember laughter, noise, gunfire, and all the romances, romances . . . The *jeune premier* and the idol of all these six estates was then, I highly recommend, (nods at DORN) Doctor Evgeniy Sergeyevich. Even now he is charming, but back then he was irresistible. Yet I am starting to be tortured by my conscience. What did I offend my poor boy for? I now feel restless.
—Kostya! Son! Kostya!

MASHA
—I will go search for him.

ARKADINA
—Please, my darling.

MASHA
—Aoo! Konstantin Gavrilovich! . . . Aoo!

(MASHA exits to the left.)

(NINA comes out from behind the platform.)

NINA
—Apparently, we are not going to continue, I may come out. Good evening! (Exchanges kisses with ARKADINA and POLINA ANDREYEVNA.)

SORIN
—Bravo! Bravo!

ARKADINA
—Bravo! Bravo! We were enamored. With such an appearance, with such a wonderful voice you cannot, it is sinful to sit in the countryside. You must have talent. Do you hear? You have to go on the stage!

NINA
—Oh, this is my dream! (Sighs.) But it will never come true.

ARKADINA
—Who knows! Now allow me to introduce you to: Trigorin, Boris Alekseyevich.

NINA
—Ah, I am so glad . . . (embarrassed) I always read you . . .

THE SEAGULL.

ARKADINA

—(seating NINA) Do not be embarrassed, my darling. He is a celebrity, but he has a simple soul. You see, he himself is embarrassed.

DORN

—I suppose we may pull up the curtain now, otherwise it is too eerie.

SHAMRAYEV

—(loudly) Yakov, pull up the curtain, my friend!

(The platform curtain goes up.)

NINA

—(to TRIGORIN) A strange play, don't you think?

TRIGORIN

—I did not understand anything. That said, I did watch it with pleasure. Your performance was quite sincere. And the decoration was beautiful.

(Pause.)

—This lake must have many fish.

NINA

—It does.

ACT ONE.

TRIGORIN
—I love fishing. There is no greater delight for me than sitting by the water in the early evening and keeping an eye on the floater.

NINA
—But I think for someone who has experienced the delight of the creative process, for him all other delights no longer exist.

ARKADINA
—(laughing) Do not talk like this. Whenever he is told nice words, he flops.

SHAMRAYEV
—I remember once at the opera theater in Moscow the famous Silva hit the *do* in the second octave. At that time, as if deliberately, a bass from our church choir was sitting in one of the cheap seats, and suddenly, you can imagine our utmost amazement, we heard from the gallery: "Bravo, Silva!"—a whole octave lower . . . Just like this: (in low bass voice) bravo, Silva . . . The theater just froze.

(Pause.)

DORN

—A quiet angel flew by.

NINA

—It is time for me to go. Good-bye.

ARKADINA

—Whither? Whither are you off to so early? We are not letting you go.

NINA

—My father is waiting for me.

ARKADINA

—What sort of person he is, really . . . (Exchanges kisses with NINA.) Well, what can we do. It's a pity, a pity to let you go.

NINA

—If you only knew how hard it is for me to leave!

ARKADINA

—Maybe somebody could walk you, my little darling.

NINA

—(frightenedly) Oh, no, no!

SORIN

—(imploringly) Stay!

ACT ONE.

NINA

—I can't, Pyotr Nikolayevich.

SORIN

—Stay for one hour and such. Why not, really . . .

NINA

—(thinks, then through tears) I can't! (Shakes SORIN's hand.)

(NINA quickly exits.)

ARKADINA

—A misfortunate girl essentially. They say her late mother passed all her huge estate to her husband, everything down to the last kopeck, and now that girl is left with nothing since her father has already willed everything to his second wife. This is outrageous.

DORN

—Yes, her father is a notorious rascal, to do him full justice.

SORIN

—(rubbing his chilled hands) Let's go as well, dear friends, it's getting humid. My legs are in pain.

ARKADINA

—It's like you've had them made out of wood, they can barely walk. Well, let's go, unlucky old man. (Takes SORIN's arm.)

SHAMRAYEV

—(holding out his arm to POLINA ANDREYEVNA) Madam?

SORIN

—I hear the dog howling again.

—Ilya Afanasyevich, would you be so kind as to order someone to untie it.

SHAMRAYEV

—I can't, Pyotr Nikolayevich, I'm afraid that thieves would sneak into the granary. I have my millet in there.

—(to MEDVEDENKO) Imagine, a whole octave lower: "Bravo, Silva!" And not even a singer, just an ordinary church chorister.

MEDVEDENKO

—Do you know how much the salary of a church chorister is?

(Everyone exits, except DORN.)

DORN

—I don't know, maybe I don't understand anything or have lost my mind, but the play did appeal to me. There was something to it. When that girl was talking about loneliness, and then when the red eyes of the devil appeared, I felt moved, and my hands trembled. It was fresh, naive... Seems it is him coming here. I would like to tell him plenty of nice things.

ACT ONE.

(TREPLEV enters.)

TREPLEV
—Everybody has already left.

DORN
—I am here.

TREPLEV
—Mashenka is searching for me all over the park. Unbearable creature.

DORN
—Konstantin Gavrilovich, your play appealed to me enormously. It was kind of strange, and I did not hear the end, but it still made a strong impression. You are a talented man, you must continue.

(TREPLEV firmly shakes DORN's hand and abruptly hugs him.)

DORN
—Pff, so nervous. Tears in your eyes . . . What was it that I wanted to say? You took the plot from the field of abstract ideas. And that is what you should have done since a literary work must certainly express some kind of grand thought. Only that which is serious is beautiful. You look so pale!

TREPLEV
—So you're saying—to continue?

DORN

—Yes... But portray only the important and the eternal. You know, I have lived a multifarious life and with some taste, I am pleased with it, but if I could experience the uplift of spirit that painters could have during the creative process, then, it seems to me, I would despise my material shell and all that is intrinsic to that shell and would carry myself away from this earth farther and higher.

TREPLEV

—Excuse me, where is Zarechnaya?

DORN

—And just one more thing. In a literary work, there must be a clear, specific thought. You must know what you are writing for, otherwise, if you take this picturesque road without a specific goal, then you will go astray, and your talent will ruin you.

TREPLEV

—(impatiently) Where's Zarechnaya?

DORN

—She went home.

TREPLEV

—(desperately) What do I do then? I want to see her... I need to see her... I will go...

(MASHA enters.)

DORN

—(to TREPLEV) Calm down, my friend.

TREPLEV

—I am still going though. I must go.

MASHA

—Go inside, Konstantin Gavrilovich. Your mother is waiting for you. She is restless.

TREPLEV

—Tell her that I left. And please, all of you, let me alone! Leave me! Do not follow me around!

DORN

—Now, now, now, dear . . . you cannot . . . That is no good.

TREPLEV

—(through tears) Good-bye, Doctor. Very grateful . . .

(TREPLEV exits.)

DORN

—(sighs) Youth, youth!

MASHA

—When there is nothing more to say, they say: youth, youth . . . (Snuffs tobacco.)

DORN

—(takes MASHA's snuffbox and tosses it into the bushes) That's disgusting!

(Pause.)

—It seems that someone is playing inside. We need to go.

MASHA

—Hold on.

DORN

—What?

MASHA

—I want to tell you one more time. I want to talk . . . (anxiously) I do not love my father . . . but my heart is set on you. For some reason, with my whole soul, I feel close to you . . . Help me then. Help me, or else I will do something silly, I will mock my life, will spoil it . . . I can no longer . . .

DORN

—What? What can I help with?

MASHA

—I suffer. No one, no one knows my suffering! (Lays her head on DORN's chest, then quietly) I love Konstantin.

DORN

—Everyone is so nervous! Everyone is so nervous! And so much love . . . Oh, the bewitching lake! (tenderly) But what is it that I can do, my child? What? What?

(Curtain.)

ACT TWO.

A croquet court. Far to the right is SORIN's house with a large terrace. Visible on the left is the lake with the sparkling sun reflecting off the water. Flower beds.

Noon. It is hot.

(To one side of the croquet court, in the shade of an old linden tree, sitting on a bench are ARKADINA, DORN, and MASHA; DORN has an open book on his knees.)

ARKADINA

—(to MASHA) Let's stand up. (Both stand up.) Stand closer. You're 22 years old, and I am nearly twice your age.
—Evgeniy Sergeyevich, which one of us is more youngish?

DORN

—You, of course.

ARKADINA

—(to MASHA) You see . . . And why? Because I work, I feel, I am busy all the time, while you keep sitting in one place, you do not live . . . And I have a rule: do not look into the future. I never think of either old age or death. What must be, will be.

MASHA

—And I have a feeling as if I had already been born long, long ago; that I am portaging my life like the endless train of a dress . . . And often there is no desire whatsoever to live. (Sits down.) Of course it is all nonsense. I just need to shake myself up, to throw it all off.

DORN

—(sings very quietly) "You confess to her, my tender flowers . . ."

ARKADINA

—Then, I am as correct as an Englishman. I, my dear, keep myself in trim, as they say, and always have my clothes and hair *comme il faut*. Would I allow myself to leave the house, even just go into the garden, wearing a blouse or without my hair styled? Never. That's why I look so kept up, because I have never been a frump, never let myself get out of hand, like some people ... (strolling along the croquet court, hands on hips) Look at me— like a pretty spring chicken. Could easily play a 15-year-old girl.

DORN

—Well, nevertheless, I continue though. (Picks up the book.) We stopped at the grocer and the rats ...

ARKADINA

—And the rats. Continue. (Sits down.) Actually, give it to me, I will read. It's my turn. (Takes the book.) And the rats ... Here it is ... "And it is assuredly as dangerous for people in good society to indulge novelists and invite them as it would be for a grocer to breed rats in his stock rooms. And yet they are loved. So, when a woman has chosen the writer she desires to conquer, she lays siege to him by means of compliments, courtesies, and accommodations ..." Well, that's how it works for the French, maybe, but we have nothing like that, none of those programs. Do me a favor, our woman ordinarily before conquering the writer must have already fallen head over ears in love. No need to look far, take, for instance, me and Trigorin ...

(SORIN, leaning on his cane, and NINA enter from the right, followed by MEDVEDENKO, pushing an empty wheelchair.)

SORIN

—(to NINA, affectionately, as if she were a child) Well? We are full of joyance? We are feeling cheerful today, after all?

—(to ARKADINA) We are full of joyance! Our father and stepmother are on their way to Tver, and we are now free for three whole days.

NINA

—(sits down by ARKADINA and hugs her) I am happy! I now belong to you.

SORIN

—(sits down in his wheelchair) She is quite adorable today!

ARKADINA

—Neatly dressed and interesting... Aren't you a clever girl. (Gives NINA a kiss.) But it is not necessary to overpraise, or we will jinx it. Where's Boris Alekseyevich?

NINA

—He is fishing by the bathing cabin.

ARKADINA

—Isn't he fed up already! (Wants to continue reading.)

ACT TWO.

NINA

—What is that?

ARKADINA

—Maupassant, *On the Water*, my little dear. (Reads several lines to herself.) Well, it is becoming uninteresting and untrue. (Closes the book.) My soul has been restless. Tell me, what's with my son? Why is he so dull and harsh? He spends whole days at the lake, and I almost never see him.

MASHA

—He does not feel so good in his soul.
—(to NINA, timidly) Please, recite something from his play!

NINA

—(shrugs her shoulders) You want me to? This is so interesting!

MASHA

—(restraining her excitement) When he himself reads something, his eyes light up, and his face turns pale. He has a beautiful, sad voice; and the manners are of a poet.

(SORIN snores.)

DORN

—(to SORIN) Good night!

ARKADINA

—Petrusha!

SORIN

—Huh?

ARKADINA

—Are you sleeping?

SORIN

—Not at all.

(Pause.)

ARKADINA

—You are not having treatment, and that is no good, my Brother.

SORIN

—I would be glad to have treatment, but the doctor does not want me to.

DORN

—To receive treatment when you are 60 years old!

ACT TWO.

SORIN

—Even when you are 60 years old, you want to live.

DORN

—(annoyedly) Eh! Then take some valerian drops.

ARKADINA

—It seems to me, it would be good for him to go to the healing waters somewhere.

DORN

—I guess, so? It is possible to go. And it is possible to not go.

ARKADINA

—Go figure.

DORN

—There is nothing to figure. Everything is clear.

(Pause.)

MEDVEDENKO

—Pyotr Nikolayevich should probably quit smoking.

SORIN

—Nonsense.

DORN

—No, that's not nonsense. Wine and tobacco depersonalize. After a cigar or a drink of vodka you are no longer Pyotr Nikolayevich, but Pyotr Nikolayevich plus someone else; your persona starts to blur, and you already relate to yourself using the third person—he.

SORIN

—(laughs) It's all right for you to deliberate. You've lived an eventful life, and me? I served in the judiciary for 28 years but have not lived yet, have not experienced anything, after all, and obviously very much want to live. You've had it all and are uninterested in life and therefore have an inclination for philosophy, whereas I want to live, and that's why I drink sherry at lunchtime and smoke cigars and such. That is all.

DORN

—You need to take your life seriously, receiving treatment when you are 60 years old, regretting that you had little pleasure in your youth, this is, excuse me, light-mindedness.

MASHA

—(stands up) Must be breakfast time. (Starts walking with a lazy, sluggish gait) My leg fell asleep . . .

(MASHA exits.)

DORN

—Time to get through a couple of drinks before breakfast.

ACT TWO.

SORIN

—There's no happiness in the poor thing's personal life.

DORN

—Nothing to be concerned about, your excellency.

SORIN

—You deliberate as a person who's had it all.

ARKADINA

—Ah, what could be more boring than this darling countryside boredom! It is hot, quiet, nobody is doing anything, everybody is philosophizing . . . It's so good being with you, my friends, it is enjoyable to listen to you, but . . . to sit in your own room and to study a part—so much better!

NINA

—(excitedly) It's so good! I understand what you mean.

SORIN

—Of course in the city is better. You are sitting in your office, the doorman does not let anyone in without approval, the telephone . . . coachmen on the street, and such . . .

DORN

—(sings quietly) "You confess to her, my tender flowers . . ."

THE SEAGULL.

(SHAMRAYEV enters, followed by POLINA ANDREYEVNA.)

SHAMRAYEV

—Here you are. Good afternoon! (Kisses ARKADINA's hand, then NINA's.) Quite glad to find you in good health.
—(to ARKADINA) My wife says that you are planning to go to the city together today. Is that true?

ARKADINA

—Yes, we are planning to.

SHAMRAYEV

—Hmm . . . This is magnificent, but how are you going to get there, dearest? Today we are moving the rye, all the workers are occupied . . . And which horses are you going to use, may I ask?

ARKADINA

—Which horses? How should I know—which horses!

SORIN

—We have the carriage horses.

SHAMRAYEV

—(anxiously) The carriage horses? And where do I get collars for them? Where do I get the collars? This is astonishing! This is incomprehensible! Dearest! Excuse me, I worship your talent, I'm willing to devote ten years of my life to you, but I cannot give you any horses!

ACT TWO.

ARKADINA

—What if I must go? What's the matter!

SHAMRAYEV

—Dearest! You do not know what it means to run a country estate!

ARKADINA

—(flaring up) That's an old story! In this case I am leaving for Moscow today. Have the horses hired for me from somebody in the village, or else I will go to the station on foot!

SHAMRAYEV

—(flaring up) In this case I am resigning from my position! Find yourself another estate manager!

(SHAMRAYEV exits.)

ARKADINA

—Every summer it's the same, every summer I am insulted here! My foot will not be set here again!

(ARKADINA exits to the left, in the direction of
the bathing cabin; one minute later she goes into the house,
followed by TRIGORIN, with fishing poles and a bucket.)

THE SEAGULL.

SORIN

—(flaring up) What disrespect! What in the devil was that! I've had enough of this, after all. Have all the horses ready at once!

NINA

—(to POLINA ANDREYEVNA) To refuse Irina Nikolayevna! A famous artist! Isn't any desire of hers, even a caprice, more important than running your estate? Simply unbelievable!

POLINA ANDREYEVNA

—(desperately) What can I do? Put yourself in my place: what can I do?

SORIN

—(to NINA) Let's go talk to my sister . . . We all will implore her not to leave. Right?
—(in the direction SHAMRAYEV went) Intolerable man! Despot!

NINA

—(to SORIN) Sit down, sit down . . . We will take you there . . . (NINA and MEDVEDENKO start pushing the wheelchair) Oh, this is so awful! . . .

SORIN

—Yes, yes, this is awful . . . But he will not quit, I will go talk to him now.

(Everyone exits, except DORN and POLINA ANDREYEVNA.)

ACT TWO.

DORN

—People are dull. Essentially your husband should be thrown out on his neck, but instead that old broad Pyotr Nikolayevich and his sister will end up apologizing to him. You will see.

POLINA ANDREYEVNA

—He sent even the carriage horses into the field. And every day there is one blunder or another. If you only knew how it worries me! I am becoming sick; you see, I am trembling . . . I cannot tolerate his rudeness. (imploringly) Evgeniy, dear, my irresistible one, take me in . . . Our time is passing, we are no longer young, and maybe at least at the end of our lives we could stop hiding, stop lying . . .

(Pause.)

DORN

—I'm 55 years old, it's already late to change someone's life.

POLINA ANDREYEVNA

—I know you're rejecting me because there are other women besides me that you're close to. It is impossible to take in everyone. I understand. Forgive me, I bore you.

(NINA appears by the house, starts picking flowers.)

DORN

—No, it's all right.

POLINA ANDREYEVNA

—I suffer from jealousy. Of course you're a doctor, and you cannot avoid seeing other women. I understand . . .

(NINA approaches DORN and POLINA ANDREYEVNA.)

DORN

—(to NINA) How are things in there?

NINA

—Irina Nikolayevna is crying, and Pyotr Nikolayevich is having another asthma attack.

DORN

—(stands up) Need to go give them both some valerian drops . . .

NINA

—(gives DORN the flowers) For you!

DORN

—*Merci bien.* (Starts walking toward the house.)

POLINA ANDREYEVNA

—(following DORN) What pretty little flowers! (by the house, in a muffled voice) Give me these flowers! Give me these flowers! (Tears up the flowers and throws them to the side.)

(DORN and POLINA ANDREYEVNA exit.)

ACT TWO.

NINA

—How strange it is to see that a famous actress is crying, and especially over such a small matter! And isn't it strange that a famous writer, the public's favorite, he is written about in all the newspapers, his portraits are being sold, he is being translated into foreign languages, and yet he is spending the whole day catching fish and is glad that he has got two carp. I thought that famous people were proud, unapproachable, that they despised the crowd, and, with their fame and the glamour of their name, they somehow took revenge against the crowd's preference, above all, for provenance and wealth. But instead they are crying, fishing, playing cards, laughing, and being angry, like everyone else . . .

(TREPLEV enters, hatless, with a rifle and a killed seagull.)

TREPLEV
—You're alone here?

NINA
—Alone.

(TREPLEV lays the seagull at NINA's feet.)

NINA
—What does this mean?

THE SEAGULL.

TREPLEV
—I've been despicable enough to kill this seagull today. I am laying it at your feet.

NINA
—What's with you? (Picks up the seagull and keeps looking at it.)

(Pause.)

TREPLEV
—Soon in the same fashion I will kill myself.

NINA
—I do not recognize you.

TREPLEV
—Right, ever since I've stopped recognizing you. You've changed toward me, your gaze is chilling, my presence constrains you.

NINA
—Latterly you've become irritable, keep expressing yourself unintelligibly, with some sorts of symbols. And this seagull here is probably a symbol too, but forgive me, I do not understand . . . (Lays the seagull on the bench.) I am too simple to understand you.

TREPLEV

—It all started that evening when my play so foolishly flopped. Women do not forgive nonsuccess. I've burned everything, everything down to the last little piece. If you only knew how unhappy I am! Your coldness is awful, unbelievable, like I woke up and saw that this lake had suddenly dried up, or that it had drained into the ground. You've just said that you're too simple to understand me. Oh, what is there to understand! The play did not appeal to you, you despise my inspiration, already consider me unexceptional, some kind of nothingness, like so many others . . . (Stomps his foot.) I understand that so well, so well! It's like there's a nail in my brain, curse that nail as well as my own ego, which is sucking my blood out, sucking it out like a snake . . .

(TRIGORIN appears, reading his notebook.)

TREPLEV

—There's the true talent walking; stepping like Hamlet and with a notebook too. (mocking) "Words, words, words . . ." That sun has not approached you yet, but you're already smiling, your gaze has melted in its rays. I am not going to interfere.

(TREPLEV quickly exits.)

THE SEAGULL.

TRIGORIN

—(writing in the notebook) Snuffs tobacco and drinks vodka ... Always wears black. Loved by the teacher ...

NINA

—Good afternoon, Boris Alekseyevich!

TRIGORIN

—Good afternoon. The circumstances have unexpectedly made it so that it seems we're leaving today. It's unlikely we will ever see each other again. That's a pity. Not often do I have a chance to meet young women, young and interesting, I've already forgotten and cannot clearly imagine for myself how it feels to be 18, 19 years old, and that's why young women in my novels and short stories are ordinarily fake. I would really want even if only for one hour to be in your place, to find out how you think and altogether what kind of person you are.

NINA

—And I would want to be in your place.

TRIGORIN

—What for?

NINA

—To find out how a famous, talented writer feels. How does fame feel to you? How do you perceive being famous?

ACT TWO.

TRIGORIN

—How? Must be no different. I've never thought about that. (Thinks.) Must be one of the two: either you're exaggerating my fame, or it is altogether not being perceived as anything at all.

NINA

—What if you read about yourself in the newspapers?

TRIGORIN

—When praised, it feels good, and when berated, then for the next two days I feel myself in low spirits.

NINA

—A wonderful world! How I envy you, if you only knew! Different people have a different luck of the draw. Some barely carry on a boring, unnoticeable existence, all resembling one another, all unhappy; while others like, for instance, you—you are one in a million—draw a life that is interesting, bright, full of meaning ... You are happy ...

TRIGORIN

—Me? (shrugging his shoulders) Hmm ... Here you're talking about fame, about happiness, about some kind of bright, interesting life, but to me all these nice words are, forgive me, so much like marmalade that I never eat. You're very young and very kind.

NINA

—Your life is beautiful!

TRIGORIN

—What is particularly good about it? (Looks at his watch.) I must go now and write. Excuse me, I don't have time . . . (Laughs.) You, as they say, have stepped on my most favorite corn, and now I'm starting to feel anxious and a little bit angry. That said, let us talk. We will talk about my beautiful, bright life . . . Well, where do we start? (Thinks awhile.) There exist presentations that force themselves on the mind, causing a person to think day and night only about, for instance, the moon, and I have my own such moon. Day and night I'm overwhelmed by one haunting thought: I must write, I must write, I must . . . I've barely finished one novel, but already, for some reason, I must start writing another, then a third, and after the third, a fourth . . . I write uninterruptedly, as if I'm traveling in a stagecoach, and cannot do otherwise. What is it here that is beautiful and bright, I ask you? Oh, what a wild life! Here I am with you, I am anxious, but meanwhile every moment I remember that waiting for me is an unfinished novel. I see a cloud over there shaped like a grand piano. I'm thinking: need to mention somewhere in a short story that sailing along was a cloud shaped like a grand piano. It smells of heliotrope. Right away I'm making a mental note: the overly sweet smell, a widow's color, to mention in the description of a summer evening. I'm catching myself and you at every phrase, at every word and rushing in a hurry to lock up all these phrases and words in my literary treasure trove: they could possibly be useful! When I finish my work, I run to the theater or to fish; that would be a good place to rest, to doze off, but—no, there's already a heavy iron cannonball rolling over inside my head—a new plot, and I'm already being drawn to the desk, and there's the need to rush again to write and write. And it is always like that, always, and there's no peace within myself, and I feel that I'm eating away at my own life, that for the honey which I give away to someone out there, I'm depleting the pollen of my best flowers, ripping these same flowers out, and stomping on their roots. Am I not crazy? Do my friends and acquaintances conduct themselves with me as if I were sane? "What have you been writing now and then? What are you planning to gift us with?" It is always the same thing, always the same thing, and to me this attention of acquaintances, praises, admiration—all this seems to be a deception, I'm being tricked like a mentally ill person, and sometimes I'm afraid that they will suddenly sneak up behind my back, grab me, and carry me off, like Poprishchin, to the madhouse. But in those years, in my youngest, my best years, when I was starting out, writing was one continuous torture. A minor writer, especially when he is not having much luck, seems to himself clumsy, awkward, extraneous, his nerves are tense, twitching; desperately wanders he around people involved in literature and art, unaccepted, unnoticed by anyone, afraid to look straight and boldly into people's eyes, just like a passionate gambler out of money. I did not see my readers, but for some reason in my imagination they appeared to me as unfriendly, mistrustful. I was afraid of the public, they scared me, and when I had to put on my new play, every time it seemed that all brunets had a hostile sentiment while all blonds were chillingly uninterested. Oh, that was so awful! That was such torture!

NINA
—Allow me, but don't inspiration and the creative process themselves give you uplifting, happy minutes?

TRIGORIN

—They do. When I'm writing, it feels good. And reading the proofs feels good, but . . . something has barely come off the press, and I cannot tolerate it and already see that it is not what I had hoped, a mistake, that I should not have written it in the first place, and I feel annoyed, and my soul feels like rubbish . . . (laughing) All the while the public is saying: "Ha, amusing, talented . . . Amusing, but a long way to Tolstoy," or: "A beautiful piece, but *Fathers and Sons* by Turgenev is better." And to the grave it will only be amusing and talented, amusing and talented— and nothing else, and when I die, my acquaintances walking by my graveside will say: "Here lies Trigorin. A good writer was he, but he wrote worse than Turgenev."

NINA

—Forgive me, I refuse to understand you. You are simply spoiled by success.

TRIGORIN

—By which success? I've never liked myself. I don't love myself as a writer. The worst of it all is that I am in some kind of delirium and often do not understand what I'm writing . . . I love this water here, the trees, the sky, I feel nature, it arouses within me a passion, the insurmountable desire to write. But I am not a landscape writer alone, I am also a citizen, I love my homeland, the people, I feel that if I am a writer, then I am obliged to talk about the people, about their sufferings, about their future, to talk about science, about human rights, and so on and so forth, and

I end up talking about everything, rushing, being urged on from all sides, everyone is angry with me, I'm darting from one side to another, like a fox cornered by hounds, I see that life and science keep moving more and more forward, yet I keep falling farther and farther behind, like someone from the countryside who has missed his train, and in the end I feel that I can write only about landscape, and as for everything else I am fake and fake down to the marrow of my bones.

NINA

—You've overworked yourself, and you have no time or desire to realize your significance. You may be dissatisfied with yourself, but for others you are grand and gorgeous! If I were such a writer like you, then I would give my whole life away to the crowd, but I would realize that their only happiness would be in looking up to me, and they would carry me in a chariot.

TRIGORIN

—Now, in a chariot . . . am I Agamemnon, or something?
(Both smile.)

NINA

—For the happiness of being a writer or an artist, I would tolerate nonlove of relatives, absence of necessities, disappointment, I would live under just a rooftop and would eat only rye bread, would suffer from dissatisfaction with myself, from the realization of my own imperfections, but in exchange I would demand fame . . . real, resounding fame . . . (Covers her face with her hands.) My head is spinning . . . Oof! . . .

THE SEAGULL.

ARKADINA

—(offstage, from inside the house) Boris Alekseyevich!

TRIGORIN

—They're calling for me . . . Must be to pack. (Looks at the lake.) And I don't feel like leaving. Look at this, what a blessing! . . . It's so good!

NINA

—You see on the other side, there's a house and a garden?

TRIGORIN

—Yes.

NINA

—That's the estate of my late mother. The place where I was born. I've spent my whole life by this lake and know its every little island.

TRIGORIN

—It's so good here! (Notices the seagull.) And what is that?

NINA

—A seagull. Konstantin Gavrilovich killed it.

TRIGORIN

—A beautiful bird. Really, I don't feel like leaving. (Writes something in the notebook.)

NINA

—What is that you are writing?

ACT TWO.

TRIGORIN

—Nothing, just jotting down . . . Had an idea for the plot . . . (hiding the notebook) An idea for the plot of a short story: by a lake since her childhood lives a young woman, someone like you; loves the lake, like a seagull, and is happy and free, like a seagull. But by chance came along a man, saw her, and because of nothing to do destroyed her, just like this seagull.

(Pause.)

(ARKADINA appears in a window of the house.)

ARKADINA

—Boris Alekseyevich, where are you?

TRIGORIN

—(to ARKADINA) One minute! (Starts walking toward the house, glances back at NINA.)
—(to ARKADINA, by the window) What?

ARKADINA

—We are staying.

(TRIGORIN goes into the house.)

NINA

—(Approaches the front of the stage; contemplates for a while.) A dream!

(Curtain.)

ACT THREE.

The dining room in SORIN's house. Doors to the right and to the left. A buffet, a medicine chest, a table in the middle of the room. A suitcase, cardboard boxes, and other signs of an upcoming departure.

THE SEAGULL.

(TRIGORIN is having breakfast, MASHA stands by the table.)

MASHA

—I am telling you all this because you are a writer. Maybe you can benefit from it. Honestly: if he had wounded himself seriously, then I would not have lived a single minute. And yet I am courageous. Thought about it and decided: will rip this love out of my heart, will rip it out by the roots.

TRIGORIN

—And how will you do that?

MASHA

—By getting married. To Medvedenko.

TRIGORIN

—Is that the teacher?

MASHA

—Yes.

TRIGORIN

—Not sure I understand what the need is.

MASHA

—To love hopelessly, to wait years on end for something... And as soon as I am married, love will be the last thing on my mind, new troubles will drown out everything old. And at least, you know, it will be a change. Why don't we have another one?

TRIGORIN

—Wouldn't that be too much?

MASHA

—What! (Pours out a drink for each.) Don't look at me like that. Women drink more often than you think. The minority drinks openly, as I do, while the majority hides it. That's right. And always vodka or cognac. (Clinks glasses with TRIGORIN.) Here's to you! You are a simple person, it is a pity to see you leave. (Both drink.)

TRIGORIN

—I myself don't feel like leaving.

MASHA

—Then why not ask her to stay.

TRIGORIN

—No, she will not stay now. Her son is behaving extremely tactlessly. First he shoots himself, and now they say he is planning to challenge me to a duel. And what for? He is pouting, snorting, preaching new forms . . . But there's plenty of room for everyone, both the new and the old—why push and shove?

MASHA

—Well, there is jealousy too. Anyway, that is none of my business.

(Pause.)

(YAKOV, with a suitcase, enters by the left door and crosses the room; NINA enters and stops by a window.)

MASHA

—My teacher is not all that smart, but is a kind person and poor, and loves me dearly. He is pitiful. And his old woman is pitiful. Well, allow me to wish you all the best. Don't think badly of me. (Firmly shakes TRIGORIN's hand.) Very grateful for your kind disposition. Do send me your books, certainly with your autograph. But instead of "To dearest Marya Ilyinichna," write something simple like: "To Marya, who does not remember where she came from, who does not know what she is living in this world for." Good-bye!

(MASHA exits.)

NINA

—(holding out a closed fist to TRIGORIN) Odd or even?

TRIGORIN

—Even.

NINA

—(sighs) No. There is only one pellet in my hand. The question was: do I become an actress or not? Maybe someone could advise me.

TRIGORIN

—That's not the topic to ask advice about.

(Pause.)

ACT THREE.

NINA

—We are saying our good-byes and ... perhaps will never see each other again. I ask you to accept this small medallion as a remembrance of me. I ordered it engraved with your initials ... and this side with the title of your book: *Days and Nights*.

TRIGORIN

—How graceful! (Kisses the medallion.) An adorable gift!

NINA

—Once in a while think of me.

TRIGORIN

—I will think of you. I will think of you the way you were on that clear day—remember?—when you had a luminous dress ... we were talking ... and on the bench back then there was a white seagull.

NINA

—(contemplatively) Yes, a seagull ...

(Pause.)

—We cannot talk any longer, someone is coming ... Before departing give me two minutes, I implore you ...

(NINA exits to the left.)

THE SEAGULL.

(ARKADINA and SORIN, wearing an evening tailcoat with a star of an order, enter from the right, then YAKOV, preoccupied with packing.)

ARKADINA

—Why don't you, old man, stay home. You think it is a good idea to go out making visits with that rheumatism of yours?
—(to TRIGORIN) Who was that who just walked out? Nina?

TRIGORIN

—Yes.

ARKADINA

—*Pardon*, we interfered . . . (Sits down.) It seems I have everything packed. Have worn myself out.

TRIGORIN

—(reads from the medallion) *Days and Nights*, page 121, lines 11 and 12.

YAKOV

—(to TRIGORIN, while clearing the table) Do I pack your fishing poles too?

ACT THREE.

TRIGORIN
—Yes, I will need them later. As for the books, give them away to someone.

YAKOV
—Will do.

(YAKOV exits.)

TRIGORIN
—(to himself) Page 121, lines 11 and 12. What do these lines say?
—(to ARKADINA) Are there any of my books here in the house?

ARKADINA
—In my brother's office, the corner bookcase.

TRIGORIN
—(to himself) Page 121 . . .

(TRIGORIN exits.)

ARKADINA

—Really, Petrusha, maybe you could stay home . . .

SORIN

—You both are leaving, it would be hard for me at home when you are gone.

ARKADINA

—And what's in the city?

SORIN

—Nothing special, but still. (Laughs.) The foundation stone of the city hall will be laid and such . . . I want to rise up even if only for an hour or two from this little gudgeon's life, I've been lying around for much too long, like an old cigarette holder. I've ordered to have the horses ready by one, we will leave at the same time.

(Pause.)

ARKADINA

—Well, keep on living here then, don't be bored, do not catch a cold. Watch over my son. Keep him safe. Mentor him.

(Pause.)

ACT THREE.

ARKADINA

—I am about to leave and will never know why Konstantin shot himself. It seems to me, the foremost reason was jealousy, and the sooner I take Trigorin away the better.

SORIN

—How can I say it? There were other reasons too. Obviously, a young man, intelligent, lives in the country, far from the bustle of life, with no money, no status, no future. Not busy with anything. Ashamed and afraid of his indolence. I love him enormously, and he is attached to me, but after all, in the end, it seems to him that he is an extraneous person in the house, that he is a freeloader here, a parasite. Obviously, his ego . . .

ARKADINA

—He brings me grief! (contemplatively) Maybe he could enter the civil service, or something . . .

SORIN

—(quietly whistles, then indecisively) It seems to me, the best thing would be if you . . . gave him a little money. First of all he needs to dress like a normal person and such. Look, he has been wearing the same little jacket for three years, walking around without a coat . . . (Laughs.) And it wouldn't do the young man any harm to go out more . . . Maybe go abroad, or something . . . It really does not cost much.

ARKADINA

—Still . . . Perhaps I could help with new attire, but as for abroad . . . No, at the present time I cannot even help with new attire. (decisively) I do not have any money!

(SORIN laughs.)

ARKADINA

—Nyet!

SORIN

—(quietly whistles) What else. Forgive me, my dear, do not be angry. I believe you . . . You are a magnanimous, honorable woman.

ARKADINA

—(through tears) I do not have any money!

SORIN

—Had I any money, then obviously I would give him some myself, but I don't have anything, not even five kopecks. (Laughs.) The estate manager takes my entire pension away from me and spends it all on agriculture, stockbreeding, beekeeping, and my money is wasted for nothing. Bees fall off, cows die off, no one ever gives me any horses . . .

ACT THREE.

ARKADINA

—Yes, I have some money, but I am an artist; the outfits alone make me go broke.

SORIN

—You are kind, nice . . . I respect you . . . Yes . . . But something is odd with me again . . . (Wobbles a little.) My head is spinning. (Holds on to the table.) I do not feel so good and such.

ARKADINA

—(frightenedly) Petrusha! (holding SORIN up) Petrusha, my dear . . . (screaming) Help me! Help! . . .

>   (TREPLEV, with a bandage on his head, and
>   MEDVEDENKO enter.)

ARKADINA

—He does not feel so good!

SORIN

—Never mind, never mind . . . (Smiles and drinks water.) It is already gone . . . and all . . .

TREPLEV

—Do not be frightened, Mother, it is not dangerous. It happens to Uncle often these days.

TREPLEV

—Uncle, you need to lie down.

SORIN

—For a little bit, yes . . . I am still going to the city though . . . Will lie down for a little and then go . . . obviously . . . (Starts walking, leaning on his cane.)

MEDVEDENKO

—(supports SORIN by the arm) A riddle for you: in the morning on four, at noon on two, and in the evening on three . . .

SORIN

—(laughs) Exactly. And at night on his back. Very grateful to you, I can walk by myself . . .

MEDVEDENKO

—Here we go, ceremonies again! . . .

(SORIN and MEDVEDENKO exit.)

ACT THREE.

ARKADINA

—He frightened me for once!

TREPLEV

—It is unhealthy for him to live in the country. He is miserable here. Now if you, Mother, could suddenly be overgenerous and lend him one and a half, two thousand rubles, then he would be able to live in the city for one whole year.

ARKADINA

—I have no money. I am an actress, not a bank-tress.

(Pause.)

TREPLEV

—Mother, change my bandage. You do that well.

ARKADINA

—(takes iodoform and the box of bandaging supplies from the medicine chest) And the doctor is late.

TREPLEV

—Promised to be here by ten, and it's already noon.

ARKADINA

—Sit down. (Removes the old bandage from TREPLEV's head.) You look like you're in a turban. Yesterday some visitor asked in the kitchen what nationality you were. What you have here has almost completely healed up. Only some nonsense left. (Kisses TREPLEV on the head.) While I am gone, you are not going to do tchick-tchick again, are you?

TREPLEV

—No, Mother. That was a minute of insane desperation when I could not possess my faculties. It will not be repeated. (Kisses ARKADINA's hand.) You have golden hands. I remember once, ages ago, when you were still serving in the state theater—I was little then—there was a fight in our courtyard, and a washerwoman was badly beaten. Remember? She was picked up unconscious . . . you kept visiting her, bringing her medicine, bathing her children in the washtub. You really don't remember?

ARKADINA

—No. (Starts putting a new bandage on.)

TREPLEV

—Two ballerinas lived in the same building as us at that time . . . They would visit you to have some coffee . . .

ARKADINA

—That I remember.

TREPLEV
—Quite devout they were.

(Pause.)

—Latterly, these last few days, I love you as tenderly and selflessly as I did in childhood. Other than you, now I do not have anyone else left. Only why, why have you succumbed to the influence of that man?

ARKADINA
—You do not understand him, Konstantin. That is the most honorable character . . .

TREPLEV
—Yet when it was reported to him that I was planning to challenge him to a duel, that honor did not prevent him from behaving like a coward. He is leaving. What a shameful flight!

ARKADINA
—What nonsense! I myself am asking him to leave this place.

TREPLEV
—The most honorable character! Here we are almost fighting over him, while he is now somewhere in the living room or out in the garden laughing at us . . . cultivating Nina, trying to thoroughly convince her that he is a genius.

ARKADINA

—It must be a delight for you to tell me unpleasantries. I respect that man and ask that in my presence you do not talk about him poorly.

TREPLEV

—And I do not respect him. You want me to look up to him as a genius, but forgive me, I am not able to lie, his writings disgust me.

ARKADINA

—That's envy. People with no talent but only claims have nothing else left to do but reprehend real talents. Like some sort of consolation!

TREPLEV

—(ironically) Real talents! (resentfully) I am more talented than all of you, for that matter! (Tears off the new bandage from his head.) You, the slaves to routine, have highjacked the precedence in art and consider legitimate and real only what you do yourselves, and everything else you oppress and stifle! I do not accept any of you! Neither you nor him!

ARKADINA
—Decadent! . . .

TREPLEV

—Take off to your cute theater and perform in pitiful, worthless plays!

ARKADINA

—Never have I performed in such plays. Let me alone! You have no capacity to write even a pitiful vaudeville. A tradesman from Kiev! Parasite!

TREPLEV

—Skinflint!

ARKADINA

—Rags!

(TREPLEV sits down and starts crying quietly.)

ARKADINA

—Nothingness! (Walks anxiously.) Do not cry. It is not necessary to cry . . . (ARKADINA starts crying.) There's no need . . . (Kisses TREPLEV on the forehead, cheeks, head.) My darling child, forgive me . . . Forgive your sinful mother. Forgive an unhappy woman.

TREPLEV

—(hugs ARKADINA) If you only knew! I've lost everything. She does not love me, and I already cannot write . . . all my hopes have vanished . . .

THE SEAGULL.

ARKADINA

—Do not despair... Everything will work out. He is going to leave now, she is going to love you again. (Wipes away TREPLEV's tears.) That is enough. We have already made peace.

TREPLEV

—(kisses ARKADINA's hands) Yes, Mother.

ARKADINA

—(tenderly) Make peace with him too... There is no need for a duel... There is no need, right?

TREPLEV

—Right... Only, Mother, allow me to not see him. It is hard for me... beyond my strength...

(TRIGORIN enters with his book.)

TREPLEV

—(to ARKADINA) That's... I will leave... (Quickly puts the medical supplies back into the medicine chest.) And then the doctor will take care of the bandaging...

TRIGORIN

—(to himself) Page 121... lines 11 and 12... Here it is... "If you ever need my life, then come along and take it."

(TREPLEV picks up the bandage from the floor and exits.)

ACT THREE.

ARKADINA

—(looks at her watch) The horses will be ready soon.

TRIGORIN

—(to himself) If you ever need my life, then come along and take it.

ARKADINA

—You have, I hope, everything packed by now?

TRIGORIN

—(to ARKADINA, impatiently) Yes, yes . . .
—(to himself, contemplatively) Why in that pure soul's calling did I hear sadness, and why did my heart shrink so painfully? . . . If you ever need my life, then come along and take it.
—(to ARKADINA) Let's stay one more day!

(ARKADINA shakes her head.)

TRIGORIN

—Let's stay!

ARKADINA

—Darling, I know what's holding you here. But exert some power over yourself. You've become a bit tipsy, sober up.

TRIGORIN

—Be sober too, be intelligent, be judicious, I implore you, look at all this as a true friend . . . (Shakes ARKADINA's hand.) You are able to make sacrifices . . . Be my friend, let me go . . .

ARKADINA

—(very anxiously) Are you so infatuated?

TRIGORIN

—I am mesmerized by her! It may be that this is exactly what I need.

ARKADINA

—The love of a provincial girl? Oh, how little you know yourself!

TRIGORIN

—Sometimes people sleep while they're walking, and now I am talking to you, but I feel as if I am sleeping and see her in my dream . . . I've been overcome by sweet, wonderful dreams . . . Let go . . .

ARKADINA

—(trembling) No, no . . . I am an ordinary woman, you must not talk to me like this . . . Do not torture me, Boris . . . I am scared . . .

TRIGORIN

—If you want to, you can be extraordinary. Love that is young, adorable, poetic, that carries you away into the world of fantasies— on this earth it is the only one that can bring happiness! I have not experienced such love before . . . There was never the time in my youth, I was beating down editors' doors, fighting for necessities . . . Now it is, this kind of love, it is here at last, it is mesmerizing me . . . What's the point of running away from it?

ACT THREE.

ARKADINA

—(resentfully) You've gone insane!

TRIGORIN

—So be it.

ARKADINA

—You all have conspired to torture me today! (Starts crying.)

TRIGORIN

—(puts his head in his hands) She doesn't understand! She doesn't want to understand!

ARKADINA

—Am I really so old and ugly already that you can talk to me without embarrassment about other women? (Hugs and kisses TRIGORIN.) Oh, you have lost your mind! My beautiful, wonderful . . . You are the last page of my life! (Kneels down.) My joy, my pride, my blessing . . . (Hugs TRIGORIN's knees.) If you abandon me, even if only for one hour, then I will not be able to go on living, I will go insane, my amazing, magnificent, my master . . .

TRIGORIN

—Someone may walk in. (Helps ARKADINA stand up.)

ARKADINA

—So be it, I am not ashamed of my love for you. (Kisses TRIGORIN's hands.) My treasure, my desperate mind, you want to behave like an insane man, but I do not want you to, I will not let you go . . . (Laughs.) You are mine . . . you are mine . . . And this forehead is mine, and the eyes are mine, and this beautiful silky hair is also mine . . . You are all mine. You are so talented, intelligent, the best of all present-day writers, you are the only hope of Russia . . . You have so much sincerity, simplicity, freshness, healthy humor . . . You can with a single stroke convey the foremost quality of a person or landscape, your characters are nearly alive. Oh, it is impossible to read you without excitement! You think this is *thymiama*? That I am flattering you? Now, look into my eyes . . . look . . . How do I resemble a liar? You see now, I am the only one who is able to appreciate you; the only one who tells you the truth, my darling, wonderful . . . You are going? Right? You are not going to abandon me, are you? . . .

TRIGORIN

—I do not have my own volition . . . I've never had my own volition . . . Sluggish, soft, always obedient—can this possibly be appealing to a woman? Take me, carry me away, just do not let me take even one step away from you . . .

ARKADINA

—(to herself) Now he is mine.

ACT THREE.

ARKADINA
—(to TRIGORIN, presumptuously, as if nothing had happened) Actually, if you want to, you may stay. I will go by myself, and you will join me later, in a week. Indeed, are you in a hurry to be somewhere?

TRIGORIN
—No, we are going together.

ARKADINA
—As you want. Together is together . . .

(Pause.)

(TRIGORIN writes something in the notebook.)

ARKADINA
—What is it?

TRIGORIN
—Heard a good expression this morning: "Maidens' pinewood . . ." Could be useful. (Stretches a little.) That means we're going? More trains, stations, restaurants, cutlets, conversations . . .

(SHAMRAYEV enters. While SHAMRAYEV is talking, YAKOV enters, bustling with the suitcases; MAID enters with ARKADINA's hat, manteau, umbrella, and gloves; everyone helps ARKADINA dress; COOK peeks out from behind the left door, then enters indecisively; POLINA ANDREYEVNA enters with a tiny basket of plums.)

SHAMRAYEV
—I have the honor to report with regret and sorrow that the horses are ready. It is time, dearest, to go to the station; the train arrives at five minutes after two. Would you, Irina Nikolayevna, be so kind as to make an inquiry: where is the actor Suzdaltsev nowadays? Is he still alive? Is he still healthy? Used to drink together back in the day... He was inimitable in *The Mail Coach Ambush*... I remember at the same theater in Elisavetgrad there was the actor Izmaylov who specialized in tragedy, also a remarkable character... Do not rush, dearest, you still have five more minutes. Once they were playing conspirators in some melodrama, and when they were suddenly discovered, they were supposed to say: "We've been caught in a trap," but Izmaylov said—"We've been caught in a part..." (Bursts out laughing.) In a part!...

POLINA ANDREYEVNA
—(to ARKADINA) Here are some plums for the road... Very sweet. Maybe you would want to have a little treat...

ARKADINA
—You are very kind, Polina Andreyevna.

ACT THREE.

POLINA ANDREYEVNA
—Good-bye, my dear! If something wasn't quite right, then forgive me. (Starts crying.)

ARKADINA
—(hugs POLINA ANDREYEVNA) Everything has been good, everything has been good. It is not necessary to cry though.

POLINA ANDREYEVNA
—Our time is passing!

ARKADINA
—What can we do!

(SORIN, wearing a caped coat and a hat, with a walking stick, and MEDVEDENKO enter by the left door.)

SORIN
—(crossing the room) Sister, it's time, we do not want to be late, after all. I am getting into my carriage.

(SORIN exits.)

MEDVEDENKO
—And I will go to the station on foot . . . to say the last good-bye. I am quite fast . . .

(MEDVEDENKO exits.)

ARKADINA

—Until next time, my dear ones . . . If we are still alive and well, we will see one another again next year . . . (MAID, YAKOV, and COOK kiss ARKADINA's hand.) Don't forget me.
—(to COOK) Here is a ruble for the three of you.

COOK

—Our most humble thank you, our madam. We wish you a pleasant journey! Very grateful to you!

YAKOV

—Good-bye and Godspeed!

SHAMRAYEV

—(to ARKADINA) We will be only too happy to receive a little letter from you!
—Farewell, Boris Alekseyevich!

ARKADINA

—Where's Konstantin? Tell him that I'm leaving. I need to say good-bye. Well, don't think badly of me.
—(to YAKOV) I gave a ruble to the cook. That's for the three of you.

(Everyone exits through the right door. Typical departure noise offstage. MAID returns to pick up the forgotten basket of plums and exits again.)

ACT THREE.

(TRIGORIN returns.)

T R I G O R I N
—(crossing the room) I forgot my cane. It seems to be out there, on the terrace.

(NINA enters by the left door.)

T R I G O R I N
—It is you? We're leaving . . .

N I N A
—I had a feeling that we would see each other again. Boris Alekseyevich, I decided irreversibly, the card is drawn, I am going on the stage. Tomorrow I will no longer be here, I am walking out on my father, abandoning everything, starting a new life . . . I am leaving, like you . . . for Moscow. We will see each other over there.

T R I G O R I N
—(glances at the right door) Stay at the Slavyanskiy Bazar Hotel . . . Let me know right away . . . I'm at the Grokholskiy's House, Molchanovka Street . . . I'm in a hurry . . .

(Pause.)

N I N A
—One more minute . . .

TRIGORIN

—(in half voice) You are so beautiful . . . Oh, what happiness it is to think that we will see each other soon! I will again see these wonderful eyes, the inexpressibly beautiful, tender smile . . . these timid features, the expression of angelic purity . . . My dear . . . (A long kiss.)

(Curtain.)

ACT FOUR.

Two years have passed.

One of the living rooms in SORIN's house, turned into an office by TREPLEV. The doors to the right and to the left lead to other rooms. The glass door in the center leads to the terrace. Typical living room furniture as well as a writing desk in the right corner, a Turkish divan by the left door, a bookcase, books on windowsills and on chairs.

Evening. A single lamp, with a shade over it, is burning. Semidarkness. The wind is howling in the chimneys. Outside, trees are making noise, and a watchman is making the rounds with his wooden knocker.

(MEDVEDENKO and MASHA enter.)

MASHA

—Konstantin Gavrilovich! Konstantin Gavrilovich! (looking around) Everyone has left. The old man keeps asking every minute where is Kostya, where is Kostya . . . Cannot live without him . . .

MEDVEDENKO

—He is afraid of loneliness. (listening closely) What awful weather! For the second day in a row.

MASHA

—(turns up the lamp wick for more light) There are waves on the lake. Huge ones.

MEDVEDENKO

—It is dark in the garden. Probably need to ask someone to break down that theater. It is standing naked, ugly, like a skeleton, and the curtain is flapping in the wind. When I was walking by yesterday evening, it seemed to me that someone was crying.

MASHA
—Here we go . . .

(Pause.)

MEDVEDENKO

—Let's go home, Masha.

MASHA

—(shakes her head) I'm staying here tonight.

MEDVEDENKO

—(imploringly) Masha, let's go! Our little child must be hungry.

MASHA

—That's nothing. Matryona can feed him.

(Pause.)

MEDVEDENKO

—It's a pity. It's already the third night without his mother.

MASHA

—You've become so dull. At least before you used to philosophize, and now it is only the child, going home, the child, going home—and I never hear anything else from you.

MEDVEDENKO

—Let's go, Masha.

MASHA

—Go yourself.

MEDVEDENKO

—Your father will not give me a horse.

MASHA

—He will. You ask him, and he will.

MEDVEDENKO

—Perhaps I will ask. That means you would be back tomorrow?

MASHA

—(snuffs tobacco) Tomorrow, fine. Stop being a nuisance . . .

(TREPLEV, with pillows and a blanket, and POLINA ANDREYEVNA, with bedclothes, enter and lay the bedding on the Turkish divan, then TREPLEV walks to his writing desk and sits down.)

MASHA

—What is this for, Mother?

POLINA ANDREYEVNA

—Pyotr Nikolayevich asked to lay out his bed in Kostya's room.

MASHA

—Let me do it . . . (Starts making the bed.)

ACT FOUR.

POLINA ANDREYEVNA
—(sighs) An old man is twice a child . . . (Approaches the writing desk and starts looking at the manuscript while leaning on the desk.)

(Pause.)

MEDVEDENKO
—I will go then. Bye, Masha. (Kisses MASHA's hand.)
—Good-bye, Mother. (Wants to kiss POLINA ANDREYEVNA's hand.)

POLINA ANDREYEVNA
—(annoyedly) Go! Go with God.

MEDVEDENKO
—Good-bye, Konstantin Gavrilovich.

(TREPLEV silently holds out his hand for a handshake; MEDVEDENKO exits.)

POLINA ANDREYEVNA

—(looking at the manuscript) No one would have thought or could have guessed that you, Kostya, would turn into a real writer. And now, thank God, the money has started to come in from the magazines. (Runs her hand through TREPLEV's hair.) And you've become beautiful . . . My dear, nice Kostya, be a little more affectionate with my Mashenka! . . .

MASHA

—(making the bed) Let him alone, Mother.

POLINA ANDREYEVNA

—(to TREPLEV) She is an outstanding girl.

(Pause.)

—A woman, Kostya, does not need anything, just glance at her affectionately once in a while. I know a little about that myself.

(TREPLEV stands up and silently exits.)

MASHA

—Now you've made him angry. Why did you have to harass him!

POLINA ANDREYEVNA

—I feel pity for you, Mashenka.

ACT FOUR.

MASHA

—As if I need it!

POLINA ANDREYEVNA

—My heart has been aching over and over for you. I really see everything, understand everything.

MASHA

—Everything is nonsense. Hopeless love—that's only for novels. It's nothing. There's no need to let myself get out of hand though and keep waiting for something, waiting for better weather at sea . . . Once a heart is infested with love, that love needs to be got rid of. And my husband was promised a transfer to another county. As soon as we move—I will forget everything . . . will rip it out of my heart by the roots.

(A melancholic waltz is being played three rooms away.)

POLINA ANDREYEVNA

—Kostya is playing. That means he feels miserable.

MASHA

—(waltzes noiselessly two, three turns) The main thing, Mother, is to have it out of sight. I just hope they give Semyon his transfer, and then, believe me, I will forget in one month. Nothing is all it is.

(The left door opens, DORN and MEDVEDENKO enter, pushing SORIN in the wheelchair.)

MEDVEDENKO
—(to DORN) I now have six at home. And flour is 70 kopecks a pood.

DORN
—Gotta keep spinning.

MEDVEDENKO
—It's all right for you to laugh. You are rolling in money.

DORN
—Money? After 30 years of practice, my friend, a practice full of worries, when I did not belong to myself all day and all night, I was able to stash away only two thousand rubles, and even that I recently went through abroad. I do not have anything.

MASHA
—(to MEDVEDENKO) Haven't you left?

MEDVEDENKO
—(guiltily) How could I? No one will give me a horse!

MASHA
—(with bitter annoyance, in half voice) I wish my eyes could not see you!

ACT FOUR.

(The wheelchair is parked on the left; POLINA ANDREYEVNA, MASHA, and DORN sit down nearby, sad MEDVEDENKO walks to the side.)

DORN
—Looks as if you've made quite some changes! Turned a living room into an office.

MASHA
—It is more convenient for Konstantin Gavrilovich to work here. He can go into the garden whenever he feels like it and think out there.

(The watchman makes the rounds with his wooden knocker offstage.)

SORIN
—Where is the sister?

DORN
—She went to the station to greet Trigorin. She will be right back.

SORIN
—If you found it necessary to write for my sister, that means I am dangerously ill. (Keeps silent awhile.) What a story, I am dangerously ill, and meanwhile no one will give me any medicine.

DORN

—And what would you like? Valerian drops? Soda? *Cinchona*?

SORIN

—Here we go, that philosophy again. Oh, what is this punishment for! (Nods at the divan.) Is that laid out for me?

POLINA ANDREYEVNA

—For you, Pyotr Nikolayevich.

SORIN

—Very grateful to you.

DORN

—(sings quietly) "Moon sails along in the midnight-time skies . . ."

SORIN

—I want to give Kostya an idea for the plot of a novel. The novel should be titled: *The Man Who Wanted To. L'homme Qui A Voulu.* In my youth back in the day I wanted to make a writer of myself—and did not; wanted to speak beautifully—and spoke abominably: (mocking himself) "and such, after all, that is all, kind of . . ." and I remember trying and trying to conclude my jury instructions, would even break into a sweat; wanted to marry—and did not; always wanted to live in the city—and now finishing out my life in the country and such.

DORN

—Wanted to become an actual state councilor—and did.

SORIN

—(laughs) That's not something I strove for. It happened by itself.

DORN

—To express displeasure with life at 62 years old, you must admit—is not magnanimous.

SORIN

—What a stubborn man. Don't you understand, I want to live!

DORN

—This is light-mindedness. According to the laws of nature, every life must have an end.

SORIN

—You deliberate as a person who's had it all. You've had it all and therefore are uninterested in life, to you it is all the same. But even you will be scared of dying.

DORN

—The fear of death—an animal fear . . . It needs to be suppressed. Those who are consciously afraid of death are only those who believe in eternal life and who happen to be scared of their sins. But you are, first, a nonbeliever, and second—what kinds of sins do you have? You served 25 years in the judiciary—that's all there is to it.

SORIN

—(laughs) Twenty-eight . . .

(TREPLEV enters and sits down on the footrest by SORIN's feet; all this time MASHA does not take her eyes off TREPLEV.)

DORN
—We're interfering with the work of Konstantin Gavrilovich.

TREPLEV
—No, it's all right.

(Pause.)

MEDVEDENKO
—Allow me to ask you, Doctor, what city abroad did you find most appealing?

DORN
—Genoa.

TREPLEV
—Why Genoa?

DORN
—There's an excellent street crowd. When you walk out of your hotel in the evening, the whole street can be clogged with people. And you end up moving among the crowd without any specific goal, hither and thither, along a broken line, living together with it, merging with it mentally, and you're starting to believe

ACT FOUR.

that there's indeed a possibility of a single world soul, like the one performed by Nina Zarechnaya in your play back in the day. By the way, where's Zarechnaya now? Where is she, and how?

TREPLEV

—Must be in good health.

DORN

—I was told that she had started living some peculiar life. What is the matter?

TREPLEV

—That is, Doctor, a long story.

DORN

—You can make it shorter.

(Pause.)

TREPLEV

—She ran away from home and shacked up with Trigorin. You know that.

DORN

—Yes, I do.

TREPLEV

—She had a child. The child died. Trigorin fell out of love with her and returned to his previous attachments, as one would expect. Actually, he never abandoned the previous ones and because of his lack of character somehow contrived to appear both here and there. As far as I could figure out from what I knew, Nina's personal life has been a complete misfortune.

DORN

—And the stage?

TREPLEV

—Seems to be even worse. She had a debut at a summer theater near Moscow, then she left for the provinces. That was the time I did not let her out of my sight, and for a while wherever she went, I went. She kept taking lead parts, but her style was rough, tasteless, with ululations, with abrupt gestures. There were moments when she gave a scream with some talent or died with some talent, but they were only moments.

DORN

—That means therefore there is talent?

TREPLEV

—It was difficult to figure out. There must be. I saw her, but she did not want to see me, and the staff did not let me into her room. I understood her mood and did not insist on making a date.

(Pause.)

ACT FOUR.

TREPLEV

—What else is there to say? Then after I returned home, I was receiving letters from her. The letters were intelligent, warm, interesting; she did not complain, but I felt that she was deeply unhappy; every line was nothing but an aching, taut nerve. And the imagination was a little out of order. She signed her name as "The Seagull." In *Rusalka* there's the miller who keeps saying that he is the raven, and she kept repeating in her letters that she was the seagull. Now she is here.

DORN

—What do you mean—here?

TREPLEV

—In the city, at the roadhouse. It's about five days now that she has been living in a room over there. I was about to go see her, and Marya Ilyinichna went there, but she is not receiving anyone. Semyon Semyonovich would have us believe that he saw her yesterday after lunch in the field, two kilometers from here.

MEDVEDENKO

—Yes, I saw her. She was walking in the other direction, toward the city. I bowed to her, asked why she had not visited us. She said she would come by.

TREPLEV

—She will not come by.

(Pause.)

TREPLEV
—Her father and stepmother do not want to know anything about her. They've placed watchmen all over so that she doesn't go anywhere near their estate. (Walks with DORN to the writing desk.) How easy it is, Doctor, to be a philosopher on paper and yet how difficult in deed!

SORIN
—An adorable girl she was.

DORN
—What's that, your excellency?

SORIN
—I said, an adorable girl she was. Actual State Councilor Sorin was actually in love with her for a while.

DORN
—You old Lovelace.

(SHAMRAYEV laughs offstage.)

POLINA ANDREYEVNA
—Seems that everyone has arrived from the station . . .

TREPLEV
—Yes, I hear my mother.

ACT FOUR.

(ARKADINA and TRIGORIN enter, followed by SHAMRAYEV.)

SHAMRAYEV
—We all are growing older, being weathered by the elements of nature, but you, dearest, are still young... A luminous jacket, liveliness... grace...

ARKADINA
—You want to jinx me again, dull man!

TRIGORIN
—Good evening, Pyotr Nikolayevich! What is it with you getting sick all the time? That is no good!
—(notices MASHA, joyfully) Marya Ilyinichna!

MASHA
—You recognized me? (Shakes TRIGORIN's hand.)

TRIGORIN
—Married?

MASHA
—For a long time.

TRIGORIN
—Happy?

(TRIGORIN exchanges bows with DORN and MEDVEDENKO,
then approaches TREPLEV indecisively.)

TRIGORIN

—Irina Nikolayevna said that you have already forgotten yesteryear and stopped being resentful.

(TREPLEV holds out his hand to TRIGORIN for a handshake.)

ARKADINA

—(to TREPLEV) Boris Alekseyevich brought this magazine with your new short story.

TREPLEV

—(accepting the magazine from TRIGORIN) Very grateful to you. You are very obliging.

(TREPLEV and TRIGORIN sit down. While they are talking, ARKADINA and POLINA ANDREYEVNA set up a card table in the middle of the room, take out the game of loto from the bookcase; SHAMRAYEV lights candles, arranges chairs.)

TRIGORIN

—Your admirers send you a bow . . . The public in Petersburg and in Moscow is altogether taking an interest in you and keeps asking me about you. Keeps asking: what he is like, how old, brunet or blond. Everyone thinks for some reason that you are no longer young. And no one knows your real family name since you are being published under a pseudonym. You are as mysterious as the Man in the Iron Mask.

TREPLEV
—Will you be staying with us long?

TRIGORIN
—No, I think I am going to Moscow tomorrow. I need to. I am in a rush to finish a novel and then also promised to give something for an anthology. In other words—an old story. The weather has greeted me unaffectionately. The wind has been brutal. Tomorrow morning if it quiets down, I will head down to the lake to fish. Besides, I need to examine the garden and that place where—remember?—your play was performed. I have a motif ripened, just need to refresh my memory of the place of the action.

MASHA
—Father, let my husband have a horse! He needs to go home.

SHAMRAYEV
—(mockingly) A horse . . . go home . . . (sternly) You saw it yourself: we have just sent them to the station. We do not want to race them again.

MASHA
—But there are other horses . . .

(SHAMRAYEV keeps silent.)

MASHA

—(waves her hand) Dealing with you is . . .

MEDVEDENKO

—I will go on foot, Masha. Really . . .

POLINA ANDREYEVNA

—(sighs) On foot, in this weather . . . (Sits down at the card table.) Please come here, dear friends.

MEDVEDENKO

—It is only six kilometers . . . Bye . . . (Kisses MASHA's hand.)
—Good-bye, Mother. (POLINA ANDREYEVNA unwillingly holds out her hand for a kiss.)
—I would not have bothered anyone, but the little child . . . (Bows to everyone.) Good-bye . . .

(MEDVEDENKO exits guiltily.)

SHAMRAYEV

—I bet he'll be fine walking. He is no general.

POLINA ANDREYEVNA

—(knocks on the card table) Please come here, dear friends. Let's not waste time, we'll be called to dinner soon.

(SHAMRAYEV, MASHA, and DORN sit down at the card table.)

ARKADINA

—(to TRIGORIN) When the evenings start growing longer and colder, here we play the game of loto. Look at this: the ancient loto set that our late mother used to play with us when we were children. Would you want to play one round with us before dinner? (Sits down with TRIGORIN at the card table.) The game is boring, but if you're used to it, then it's all right. (Deals everyone three loto cards.)

TREPLEV

—(flipping through the magazine) Has read his own novel, but has not even cut the pages of mine. (Lays the magazine on his writing desk, then starts walking in the direction of the left door.)

ARKADINA

—And you, Kostya?

TREPLEV

—Forgive me, for some reason I don't feel like it . . . I'll go for a walk. (Kisses ARKADINA on the head as he walks by.)

(TREPLEV exits.)

ARKADINA

—The bet—ten kopecks. Put mine in for me, Doctor.

DORN

—Will do.

MASHA

—Everyone is in? I begin . . . Twenty-two!

ARKADINA

—Yes.

MASHA

—Three! . . .

DORN

—Here it is.

MASHA

—Got the three? Eight! Eighty-one! Ten!

SHAMRAYEV

—Do not rush.

ARKADINA

—How I was received in Kharkov, my goodness, my head is still spinning!

ACT FOUR.

MASHA
—Thirty-four!

(A melancholic waltz is being played offstage.)

ARKADINA
—The students gave me a standing ovation... Three flower baskets, two wreaths, and this... (Removes a brooch worn over her bust and throws it on the card table.)

SHAMRAYEV
—Yes, that's quite a thing...

MASHA
—Fifty!

DORN
—Just fifty?

ARKADINA
—I was wearing an astonishing outfit... If I know anything, it is how to dress well.

POLINA ANDREYEVNA
—Kostya is playing. He feels miserable, poor boy.

SHAMRAYEV
—The newspapers berate him so much.

MASHA

—Seventy-seven!

ARKADINA

—Who wants to pay attention.

TRIGORIN

—He is not having much luck. Still cannot hit his real tone. There's something strange, nonspecific, at times even resembling nonsense. Not a single live character.

MASHA

—Eleven!

ARKADINA

—(turns to SORIN) Petrusha, are you bored?

(Pause.)

—Asleep.

DORN

—Asleep is the actual state councilor.

MASHA

—Seven! Ninety!

ACT FOUR.

TRIGORIN

—If I lived on such an estate by a lake, would I ever start writing? I would conquer that passion within me, and all I would ever do is be out fishing.

MASHA

—Twenty-eight!

TRIGORIN

—To catch a ruff or a perch—that is such a blessing!

DORN

—But I believe in Konstantin Gavrilovich. There is something. There's something! He thinks in images, his stories are colorful, striking, and I feel them deeply. It is only a pity that he does not have any specific goals. He makes an impression, and nothing else, but you can travel only so far on an impression alone.

—Irina Nikolayevna, are you glad that you have a son who is a writer?

ARKADINA

—Imagine, I still haven't read him. There's never the time.

MASHA

—Twenty-six!

(TREPLEV quietly enters and walks to his writing desk.)

SHAMRAYEV

—Boris Alekseyevich, we still have one of your things.

TRIGORIN

—What thing?

SHAMRAYEV

—A while ago Konstantin Gavrilovich shot a seagull, and you requested that I have it mounted.

TRIGORIN

—I don't remember. (contemplatively) I don't remember!

MASHA

—Sixty-six! One!

TREPLEV

—(throws open the window, then listens closely) It's so dark! I don't understand why I feel such restlessness.

ARKADINA

—Kostya, close the window, there's a draft.

(TREPLEV closes the window.)

MASHA

—Eighty-eight!

ACT FOUR.

TRIGORIN
—This round is mine, dear friends.

ARKADINA
—(cheerfully) Bravo! Bravo!

SHAMRAYEV
—Bravo!

ARKADINA
—This man is having good luck every time and everywhere. (Stands up.) And now let's all go eat something. Our celebrity did not have lunch today. We are going to continue after dinner.
—Kostya, leave your manuscripts alone, let's go eat.

TREPLEV
—I don't want to, Mother, I'm full.

ARKADINA
—As you please.
—(wakes SORIN up) Petrusha, dinner!
—(takes SHAMRAYEV's arm) I will tell you how I was received in Kharkov . . .

(POLINA ANDREYEVNA puts out the candles, then she and DORN start pushing SORIN in the wheelchair; everyone exits through the left door, except TREPLEV who is at the writing desk.)

T R E P L E V

—(about to start writing) I've been talking so much about new forms, but now I feel that little by little I myself am slipping into a routine. "The playbill on the wall proclaimed . . . A pale face framed in dark hair . . ." Proclaimed, framed . . . This is worthless. (Crosses out a section.) I will start with the hero being woken up by the sound of rain, and everything else can go. The description of the moonlit evening is overlong and overrefined. Trigorin has developed his own tricks, it is easy for him . . . He has the neck of a shattered bottle glimmering on a dam and the blackening shadow of a mill wheel—and the moonlit night is ready, while I have the trembling light, and the quiet twinkling of the stars, and the distant sounds of a grand piano dying away in the quiet fragrant air . . . This is torturous.

(Pause.)

—Yet, I'm getting closer and closer to being convinced that it is not a matter of old or new forms, it is a matter of someone writing without thinking of any forms whatsoever, writing because it is flowing freely from the soul.

(A knock at the window by the writing desk.)

—What's that? (Looks through the window.) Cannot see anything . . . (Opens the glass door and looks out into the garden.) Someone ran down the steps. (calling out) Who's there?

ACT FOUR.

(TREPLEV exits; quickly walks across the terrace; returns in half a minute with NINA.)

T R E P L E V
—Nina! Nina!

(NINA lays her head on TREPLEV's chest, sobs restrainedly.)

T R E P L E V
—(quite touched) Nina! Nina! It is you . . . you . . . It's like I had a presentiment, all day my soul has been languishing miserably. (Removes NINA's hat and talma.) Oh, my kind, my irresistible one, she is here at last! We are not going to cry, we are not going to.

N I N A
—Somebody is here.

T R E P L E V
—No one is here.

N I N A
—Lock the doors, or they will walk in.

T R E P L E V
—No one will walk in.

NINA

—I know Irina Nikolayevna is here. Lock the doors . . .

TREPLEV

—(locks the right door with a key, approaches the left door) There's no lock. I will block it with the armchair. (Blocks the left door with the armchair.) Do not be afraid, no one will walk in.

NINA

—(looks intently at TREPLEV's face) Let me take a look at you. (looking around) It is warm, nice . . . This used to be a living room back then. Have I changed a lot?

TREPLEV

—Yes . . . You've become thinner, and your eyes have become bigger. Nina, it's kind of strange for me to see you. Why didn't you let me in? Why didn't you come by earlier? I know you've been living here for almost a week . . . Every day I went to see you several times, stood under your window like a beggar.

NINA

—I was afraid that you hated me. Every night I keep having a dream that you're looking at me and do not recognize me. If you only knew! Since my very arrival I kept walking around here . . . by the lake. Many times I was by your house but did not dare to come in. Let's sit down. (Sits down with TREPLEV.) We will sit down and talk, talk. It is nice here, warm, cozy . . . Do you hear—the wind? Turgenev has a passage: "Lucky is whoever on such nights sits in the shelter of home, who has a warm corner." I am—the seagull ... No, that's not it. (Rubs her forehead.) What was I trying to say? Yes ... Turgenev ... "And may the Lord help all homeless wanderers ..." It's nothing. (NINA sobs.)

TREPLEV
—Nina, again ... Nina!

NINA
—It's nothing, it eases my mind ... It's been two years now that I have not cried. Late yesterday evening I went into the garden to see if our theater was intact. And it is standing to this day. I started crying for the first time in two years, and I was relieved, my soul got clearer. You see, I am already not crying. (Takes TREPLEV's hand.) So, you've already become a writer ... You are a writer, I am—an actress ... And we both are now part of a cycle ... I used to live joyfully, childlike—would wake up in the morning and start singing; used to love you, dreamed of fame, and now? Early tomorrow morning I'm going to Yelets, third class ... among the ordinary men, and in Yelets educated tradesmen will be harassing me with courtesies. Life is rough!

TREPLEV
—Why Yelets?

NINA
—Took an engagement for the winter season. Time to go.

T R E P L E V

—Nina, I cursed you, hated you, tore up your letters and photographs, but every minute I realized that my soul was attached to you for eternity. I do not have the strength to unlove you, Nina. Since the time I lost you and started being published, life for me has been intolerable—I suffer . . . My youth somehow has been suddenly torn away from me, and it seems that I've already been living in this world for 90 years. I've been calling for you, kissing the ground that you walked on; no matter where I look, everywhere I'm being presented with the image of your face, that affectionate smile that used to shine upon me in the best years of my life . . .

N I N A

—(bewilderedly) Why is he talking like this, why is he talking like this?

T R E P L E V

—I am lonely, not being warmed by anyone's attachment, I feel chilly as if I were underground, and no matter what I write, it all ends up dry, stale, dreary. Stay here, Nina, I implore you, or allow me to go with you!

(NINA quickly puts on her hat and talma.)

T R E P L E V

—Nina, why? In the name of God, Nina . . .

(Pause.)

ACT FOUR.

NINA

—My horses are waiting at the gate. Don't walk me, I can walk by myself . . . (through tears) Give me water . . .

(TREPLEV gives NINA water.)

TREPLEV

—Where are you off to now?

NINA

—To the city.

(Pause.)

—Irina Nikolayevna is here?

TREPLEV

—Yes . . . On Thursday Uncle did not feel good, we telegraphed for her to come here.

NINA

—Why did you say that you had been kissing the ground that I had walked on? I need to be killed. (Leans on the writing desk.) I feel so tired! I could use some rest . . . some rest! (Lifts up her head.) I am—the seagull . . . That's not it. I am—the actress. Well, that's it!

(ARKADINA and TRIGORIN laugh offstage. NINA listens closely, then runs to the left door and looks through the keyhole.)

NINA

—He is here too . . . (coming back to TREPLEV) Well, that's it . . . It's nothing . . . Right . . . He did not believe in theater, kept laughing at my dreams, and little by little I myself stopped believing, and my spirits fell . . . And then all those troubles of love, jealousy, constant fear for the little one . . . I became petty, insignificant, performed meaninglessly . . . I did not know what to do with my hands, was not able to stand on stage, did not own my voice. You do not understand that state of being when you feel that you're performing miserably. I am—the seagull. No, that's not it . . . Remember you shot the seagull? By chance came along a man, saw something, and because of nothing to do destroyed that something . . . An idea for the plot of a short story . . . That's not it . . . (Rubs her forehead.) What was I trying to say? . . . I was talking about the stage. Now I am not like that . . . I am already a real actress, I perform with delight, with excitement, get intoxicated on stage, and feel myself beautiful. And these days, while I've been living here, I keep walking on foot, keep walking and thinking, thinking and feeling how every day my soul's strength is growing . . . And now I know, I understand, Kostya, that in our craft—it's the same whether we perform on stage or write—the main thing is not the fame, not the glamour, not what I used to dream of, but the ability to endure. Be able to carry your cross and believe. I believe, and it feels not as painful, and when I think of my calling, I am not afraid of life.

ACT FOUR.

TREPLEV

—(sadly) You have found your road, you know where you're going, while I am still racing in a chaos of fantasies and images, not knowing what for and who needs it. I do not believe and do not know what my calling is.

NINA

—(listening closely) Sh . . . I will go. Good-bye. When I become an accomplished actress, come see me. Promise? And now . . . (Shakes TREPLEV's hand.) It's already late. I can barely stand on my feet . . . I am exhausted, I want something to eat . . .

TREPLEV

—Stay, I will bring you dinner . . .

NINA

—No, no . . . Do not walk me, I can walk by myself . . . My horses are nearby . . . That means she has brought him with her? Well then, it's all the same. When you see Trigorin, do not tell him anything . . . I love him. I love him even more dearly than before . . . An idea for the plot of a short story . . . I love, love passionately, desperately love. It was so good back then, Kostya! Remember? What a clear, warm, joyful, pure life, what feelings—feelings resembling tender, elegant flowers . . . Remember? "Men, lions, eagles and partridges, horned deer, geese, spiders, silent fish that used to dwell in water, sea stars, and those not visible to the naked eye—in other words, all forms of life, all forms of life, all forms of life, having accomplished a sad circle, have faded away . . . It has already been thousands of centuries since Earth has carried a single living creature, and this poor Moon needlessly lights its lantern. In a meadow cranes no longer wake up with a scream, and May beetles can no longer be heard in linden groves . . ."

(NINA abruptly hugs TREPLEV and runs out through the glass door.)

(Pause.)

T R E P L E V
—It will be no good if someone meets her in the garden and then tells Mother. It may upset Mother . . .

(For the duration of two minutes TREPLEV silently tears up all his manuscripts and throws the pieces under the writing desk, then unlocks the right door and exits.)

D O R N
—(trying to open the left door) Strange. The door appears to be locked . . .

(DORN enters and puts the armchair back in its place.)

—A steeplechase.

ACT FOUR.

(ARKADINA and POLINA ANDREYEVNA enter, followed by YAKOV, with bottles, and MASHA, then SHAMRAYEV and TRIGORIN.)

ARKADINA

—Red wine and the beer for Boris Alekseyevich go here, on the table. We are going to play and drink. Let's sit down, my dear friends.

POLINA ANDREYEVNA

—(to YAKOV) And bring the tea at once. (Lights the candles, sits down at the card table.)

SHAMRAYEV

—(walks TRIGORIN to the bookcase) Here is the thing I was talking about earlier . . . (Takes out the mounted seagull from the bookcase.) Your request.

TRIGORIN

—(looking at the seagull) I don't remember! (Thinks.) I don't remember!

(A shot offstage on the right; everyone startles.)

THE SEAGULL.

ARKADINA

—(frightenedly) What is happening?

DORN

—Nothing. It must be something in my medical bag that burst. Do not worry.

(DORN exits through the right door, returns in half a minute.)

—Just as I thought. A vial of ether burst. (sings quietly) "Enchanted again, I am standing before you . . ."

ARKADINA

—(sitting down at the card table) Pff, I was frightened. That reminded me of . . . (Covers her face with her hands.) Even my eyes blacked out . . .

DORN

—(to TRIGORIN, flipping through the magazine) There was one article published a couple of months ago . . . a letter from America, and I wanted to ask you, among other things . . . (takes TRIGORIN by the waist and walks him to the front of the stage) . . . since I am very interested in this question . . . (one tone lower, in half voice) Take Irina Nikolayevna somewhere away from here. The fact of the matter is that Konstantin Gavrilovich has shot himself . . .

(Curtain.)

ADDITIONAL MATERIALS.

ADDITIONAL MATERIALS.

Additional materials are available on the complementary website theseagullplay.com.

CPSIA information can be obtained
at www.ICGtesting.com
Printed in the USA
LVHW070302230821
695865LV00001B/1